Housepets! Will Do It For Free

By Rick Griffin

www.housepetscomic.com

Printed by Createspace
A DBA of On-Demand Publishing LLC

Print On Demand Edition

Not much else to say other than that
Copyright © 2015 Rick Griffin

"Socrates should have written comics."
— Mark Waid

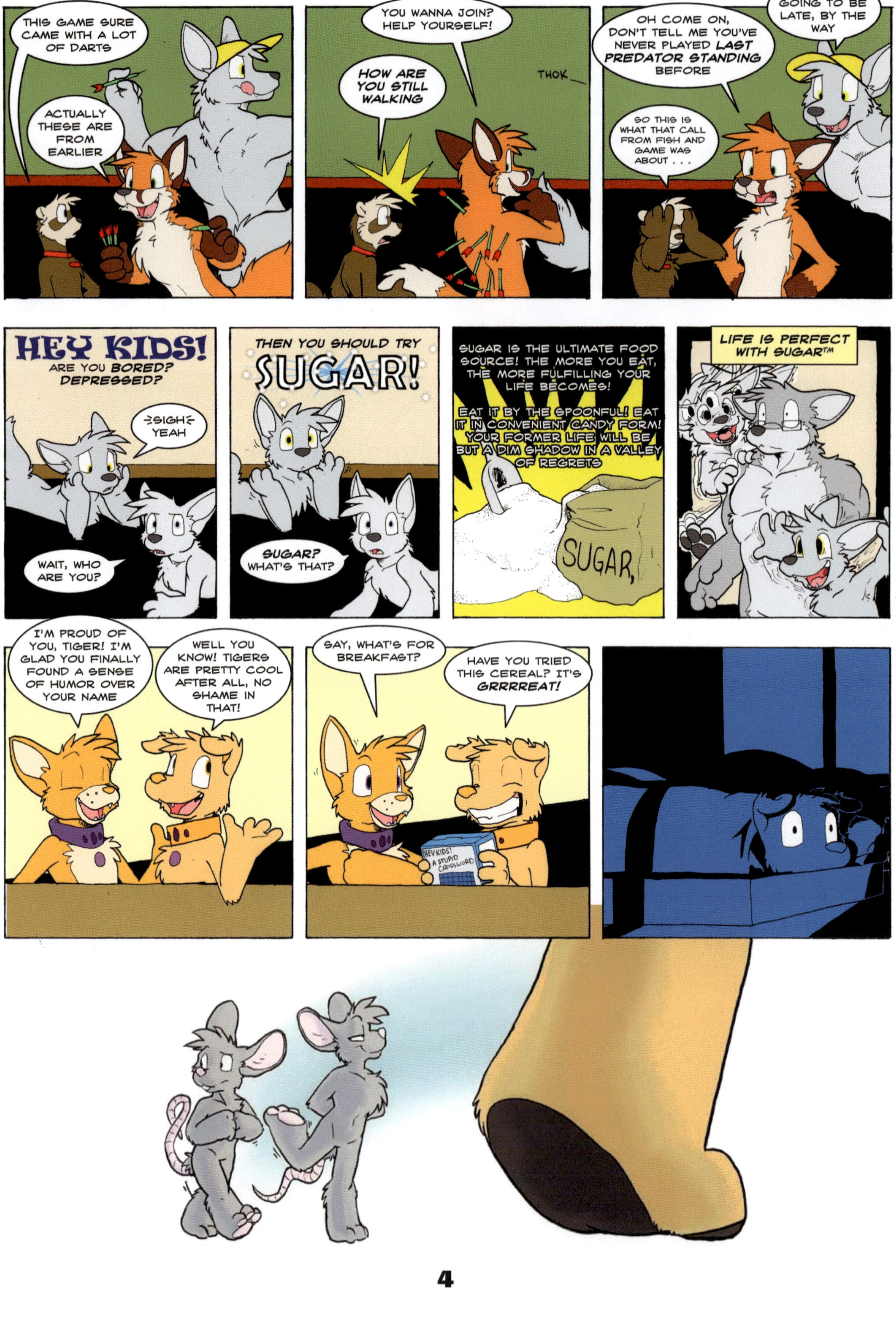

LOOK, JUST STAY HERE AND DON'T GET INTO ANY TROUBLE, OKAY?
C'MON FIDO, I NEED TO SHOW YOU THE THING!
JOEY
WHATEVS
MINIATURES
SAY, TOOTS, AREN'T *YOU* A TALL THIMBLE OF WATER
AREN'T *YOU* A LITTLE SHORT TO BE A STORMTROOPER?
WHY IS EVERYONE I MEET SUCH A MAJOR NERD CASE?
SAYS THE MOUSE WHO IMMEDIATELY CAUGHT A NERDY QUOTE
SO YOU'RE ***REALLY*** GOING WITH THAT "I ALREADY HAVE A BOYFRIEND" LINE
YES! WHAT'S SO HARD TO UNDERSTAND ABOUT THAT!
YOU CAN'T BE GIRLFRIEND TO A DOG!
WHY NOT?
C'MON, LET'S JUST YOU AND I GET TOGETHER-- ONCE YOU GO RAT YOU NEVER GO BACK!
YOU KNOW WE'RE BOTH MICE
WHAT ARE YOU, SOME KIND OF SPECIESIST?
I DON'T EVEN CARE WHAT KIND OF WEIRD JIGGY-JAMES THE STUPID BIG-NOSES PARTICIPATE IN, BUT WHAT DO YOU ***SEE*** IN THEM?
WELL . . .
EEK!
IT'S BIGGLESWORTH!
WHICH ONE?!
THE LEFT ONE ***WHY IS THAT EVEN A QUESTION***
CAREFUL CONSIDERATION OF THE SITUATION, AND NOT UNTHINKING PANIC?
COME ON GUYS I'M HUNGRY AND MOM MISCOUNTED AGAIN
ANY BRIGHT IDEAS, EGGHEAD?
YOU WANT TO KNOW WHAT I SEE IN "BIG-NOSES"?
. . . WHAT DOES THAT HAVE TO--
GOTCHA!
SQUEAK!
THAK
OOH, YOU HAVE ***REALLY*** STRONG TOES . . . PRESS A LITTLE DEEPER, HON, I CAN TAKE IT~
OKAY I COULD STAND TO GO ON A DIET OF COLD SHOWERS
I AM BOTH IMPRESSED AND APPALLED
I AM ***IMPALLED***
Mice to Meet You END!

OH, HEY GRAPE. HOW MUCH OF THAT DID YOU OVERHEAR?
ARE YOU GOING SOMEWHERE/TIME SUPER AWESOME WITH TAROT AGAIN?
BEEP
GRAPE, IT'S JUST A DATE. IT'S DINNER, A MOVIE, THE ARCADE, A WALK IN THE PARK, THE USUAL!
RIGHT!
WELL, ALRIGHT. AND YOU'RE STAYING IN TOWN?
. . . IF BY "IN TOWN" YOU MEAN "THIS TOWN, BUT IN THE GALLIFRAX DIMENSION"
I KNEW IT!
Housepets!
THE GALLIFRAX PROTOCOL
WHEN YOU AND PEANUT GO ALL THESE PLACES IT'S LIKE I'M BEING TOLD TO STAY HOME AND WATCH TV WHILE YOU'RE GOING TO A WATER PARK OR SOMETHING
NOT REALLY--THE MULTIVERSE CAN BE DANGEROUS FOR MORTALS
IS "GALLIFRAX" A DANGEROUS PLACE FOR MORTALS?
SOMETIMES
WHY GO THERE, THEN?
. . . THEY HAVE THIS AWESOME WATER PARK
YOU SEE?!
I'M TELLING YOU FOR YOUR OWN PROTECTION, NOT ALL STRANGE AEONS WERE MEANT FOR MORTAL EYES
PEANUT'S AN EXCEPTION
THAT'S UNFAIR!
IS IT UNFAIR TO KEEP YOUR SOUL FROM BEING SHATTERED ERE THE COSMOS?
DIDN'T YOU ONCE TELL US THAT ABOUT THIS UNIVERSE? HOW'S THAT COMING ALONG?
LET'S CALL IT A DOUBLE DATE
C'MON MAXIE, LET'S GO UNIVERSE SURFING
HOW DID I GET HERE
KER-FRAX
HAH! THIS PLACE LOOKS PRETTY MUCH THE SAME!
WHEN YOU SAID IT WAS STRANGE AEONS I THOUGHT YOU MEANT---
TAROT? WHY ARE YOU AS TALL AS I AM?
OKAY, WHAT GIVES
THIS WORLD HAS SOME VERY STRANGE RULES
FIRST MY EAR AND NOW MY THUMBS?!

LOOKIN' GOOD, GRAPE!
A LOT SMALLER THAN I THOUGHT, BUT GOOD
ONCE OR TWICE. FUN, HUH?
GOOD?! IT'S WEIRD!
YOU'VE DONE THIS BEFORE?
WHYYY
I'M NOT MOVING RIGHT! I FEEL ON THE EDGE OF DISLOCATING MY EVERYTHING!
JUST DON'T THINK ABOUT IT, IT COMES NATURALLY
HOW CAN YOU NOT THINK ABOUT IT?!
MAXIE, I THINK YOU'RE MISSING THE BASIC PREMISE HERE
I'LL MAINTAIN MY DIGNITY, THANK YOU VERY MUCH!
LET ME SEE IF I HAVE THIS STRAIGHT--IN THIS UNIVERSE, WE ALL MOVE AROUND LIKE HORSES
YUP!
STILL WEIRD
OOF!
I MEAN, ALL THE HOUSES LOOK NORMAL, RIGHT? HOW ARE WE EVEN SUPPOSED TO USE THE DOORS?
OH, THAT'S JUST FOR HUMANS. THEY'RE STILL THE SAME
WHAT?! WHAT MAKES HUMANS SO SPECIAL!?
YOU KNOW, I STILL HAVEN'T FIGURED THAT OUT
GREAT! NOW THIS UNIVERSE IS SPINNING! WHAT ARE WE EVEN DOING HERE?!
I KNOW IT'S STRANGE MAX, BUT IT'S WORTH IT FOR THE AWESOME WATER PARK!
OH, WE'RE NOT GOING TO THE WATER PARK, I ONLY SAID THIS UNIVERSE HAS ONE
YEAH, IT IS PRETTY AWESOME BUT WE'VE BEEN HITTING THE THEME PARKS HARD LATELY, SO--
WHERE ARE YOU GOING?!
WE WERE GOING TO SEE AIR BUD 12 AT THE DOLLAR THEATER
SHE'S A BIG GIRL NOW "DADDY", YOU GOT TO LET HER GO
I WAS HOPING GRAPE AND MAX WOULD HANG OUT BUT MEETING IN THE PARK LATER IS OKAY TOO!
ACTUALLY IT'S BETTER THEY'RE GONE, I HAVE SOMETHING KINDA SERIOUS TO TALK ABOUT LATER
TAROT! DO YOU HAVE FLEAS?
WHAT? NO!
BUT YOU'D TELL ME IF YOU DID, RIGHT?
PEANUT, YOUR BLUNT HONESTY IS USUALLY YOUR MOST ADMIRABLE QUALITY

MAX, I'M STARVING. YOU'RE LUCKY THE FISH MARKET IS IN THE SAME PLACE
DON'T WORRY GRAPE, IT'S MY RESPONSIBILITY TO SHOW A LADY A GOOD TIME
I HAVE TO WEAR THE PANTS IN THIS RELATIONSHIP
FISH MARK
MAX, EVEN IF WE WEREN'T QUADRUPEDS . . .
EXCUSE ME! I'D LIKE TO SEE YOUR FRESHEST SELECTION!
MROW MEO MEOOW
MAX, SOMETHING'S WRONG, HE CAN'T UNDERSTAND US
I NOTICED, BABE! I GOT THIS
¡OYE, CEREBRO DE BACALAO! ¡TENGO MEMORIZADA LA TARGETA DE CRÉDITO DE MI PAPÁ! ¡ATIENDEME!
GRAPE, WHERE ARE YOU GOING? THE BEST FISH IS KEPT BEHIND THE--
BOOT
SAY, THIS SETUP WOULDN'T LOOK LIKE LADY AND THE TRAMP BECAUSE YOU WANT TO RECREATE THAT SCENE, WOULD IT?
MAAAYBE
SORRY! THE SPAGHETTI'S ALL GONE, SO I MADE YOU RIGATONI, CAPICHE?
YOU KNOW, I NEVER ACTUALLY SAW THAT MOVIE
ME EITHER
Groumf
Mouf
Monf
Omf
I HAD THAT, YOU KNOW
THEY CAN'T UNDERSTAND US, DUMMY! THIS WORLD TREATS US LIKE FISH AND INSECTS
THEN DID YOU HAVE TO GET MACKEREL? HE HAD SWORDFISH UP THERE
YOU'RE LUCKY I CAN'T MAKE A FIST

FOUR FEET IS CHEATING!
YOU'RE JUST SORE 'CAUSE YOU'RE LOSING!
CAN'T YOU JUST TELL ME WHAT YOU NEED TO TALK ABOUT?
NO, PEANUT, I DON'T WANT YOU WORRYING ABOUT IT FOR THE REST OF THE DATE
BUT AS A SMALL HINT, IT HAS TO DO WITH THE GAME
AWW TAROT, YOU MADE ME LOSE!
SHHH!
MAYBE THIS WAS A MISTAKE. WE SHOULD HAVE GONE WITH PEANUT AND TAROT
DON'T BE A SOURPUSS! I KNOW WHAT'LL CHEER YOU UP!
SOMEONE'S A-ROCKING MY DREAMBOAT~
MAX . . .
HOP!
SOMEONE'S INVADING MY DREAM~
WE WERE SAILING ALONG PEACEFUL AND CALM
SUDDENLY SOMETHING WENT--
BOOT
I CAN'T STAND THE SUSPENSE! WHAT ARE YOU GOING TO TALK TO ME ABOUT?!
YOU KNOW ABOUT THE DRAGON, RIGHT?
YEAH I KNOW YOUR DRAGON FORM! IT'S AWESOME
SHE'S NOT MY "FORM", PEANUT
WE'RE SEPARATE ENTITIES
I'VE BEEN CHEATING ON YOU?!
NO!
WELL YES BUT NOT TECHNICALLY--
LOOK THIS IS WHAT I WAS TRYING TO AVOID

WHY DIDN'T YOU TELL ME?
WE DID
AND YOU WERE LIKE "OKAY" AND KEPT DOODLING A PICTURE OF A SHARK?
THEN WHY DIDN'T YOU TELL ME SO I'D LISTEN?!
YOU MEAN SHE'S HERE?
THAT'S WHAT WE'RE DOING NOW
SHE'S BEEN HERE THE WHOLE TIME
FLASH
INCIDENTALLY SHE'S VERY AGITATED ABOUT ALL THIS
AND NO PRESSURE OR ANYTHING
BUT YOU'RE GONNA HAVE TO CHOOSE BETWEEN US RIGHT NOW
HEY! SOMEONE TRASHED OUR TRASH PILE!
GASP! A RACCOON! YOU WON'T PILFER OUR GENERATIONAL TRASH PILE, YOU DISEASED RODENT!
HOW AM I EVEN SUPPOSED TO REPLY TO THAT? THERE ARE SO MANY THINGS WRONG WITH IT, I'D NEED AN ITEMIZED LIST
YOU WON'T FOOL US WITH YOUR MIND GAMES, EITHER!
PEANUT, I CANNOT BEAR THIS ANY LONGER--IT IS I WHO LOVE YOU, DEEPLY AND TRULY
WE WENT ON ONE DATE
BUT IT WAS I WHO GAVE YOU THOSE GIFTS, LIKE YOUR TELEPATHIC BOND
WHATEVER HAPPENED TO THAT ANYWAY?
THAT'S THE PROBLEM. DRAGON'S BICKERING WITH ME TURNED INTO FIGHTING, AND THAT WEAKENS OUR BOND IN TURN
HAVEN'T YOU NOTICED MY FUTURE SIGHT HAS BEEN OFF LATELY?
I THOUGHT YOU WERE JUST TURNING NORMAL
THAT IS . . . I'M GOING TO HIDE BEHIND THOSE BUSHES TO THINK?

-SIGH-
MISS DRAGON, I DO REALLY LIKE YOU AND ALL
BUT I DON'T KNOW YOU SO I CAN'T VERY WELL "CHOOSE" YOU OVER TAROT, YOU KNOW?
RIGHT?
IMPUDENCE!
YOU TURN DOWN A BEING OF THE HEAVENLY ORDER?
YOU CANNOT FATHOM WHAT I'LL--
--I'LL--
WAAAAAH-HAAA-AAAH!
KRAKKOOOOOM!
SHE'S TAKING THIS MUCH BETTER THAN I THOUGHT
I HAD THAT
THEN YOU SURE PULLED A CONVINCING STAGE SHOW--WAS THE FACE-CHEWING CHOREOGRAPHED, OR WAS IT IMPROV?
LOOK, WE'RE FINE! AT LEAST THINGS CAN'T--
KRAKKOOM!
I WASN'T GONNA SAY IT!
WHAT IS GOING ON HERE?!
OKAY SO THIS DRAGON IS A DEMIGOD THING AND IS THE SOURCE OF TAROT'S SUPERPOWERS AND SHE WANTED ME TO BE HER BOYFRIEND BUT I SAID NO CAUSE THAT'D BE WRONG AND THIS ALL HAPPENED AND NOW I DON'T KNOW WHAT TO DO!
WHAT?!
NO
I'VE SEEN SOME CARP IN THIS PLACE BUT THIS IS UTTERLY RIDICULOUS!
HAS EVERYTHING BEEN HER DOING?! CAN'T SHE DO EVERYTHING?!
WHAT DOES SHE HAVE TO MOURN?!
HOW CAN A GOD EVEN CLAIM TO KNOW WHAT PAIN IS?!
TO KNOW WHAT IT'S LIKE NOT TO LOSE, BUT TO SINK TO THE BOTTOM?!
HOW CAN A GOD KNOW WHAT IT FEELS LIKE
WHEN IT'S NOT CIRCUMSTANCES OR INTERFERENCE OR EVEN ALL THE BAD LUCK
BUT BECAUSE YOU'RE NOT GOOD ENOUGH FOR THE ONE YOU LOVE
BECAUSE YOU'RE NOT GOOD ENOUGH FOR ANYONE
GREAT, I POUR MY HEART OUT AND I GET THE OUTER LIMITS ENDING

Panel 1: (Pete hopping excitedly)

Panel 2: (Sign on door: "PRINCESSES AND UNICORNS ONLY" / "DO NOT COME IN PETE!")

Panel 3: (Signs: "WE HAVE ALREADY WON", "LOVE AND DEVOTION", "LOVE IS THE ETERNAL ANSWER")

Panel 4:
- SORRY FOR YELLING, MA'AM
- 'SOKAY, I'M USED TO IT
- THE FOUR-LEGGED WORLD IS WEIRD. IT KINDA GOT TO ME

Panel 5:
- I KNOW. I'M SORRY
- WE'RE NEVER QUITE PREPARED TO UNDERSTAND THE STRUGGLE OTHERS GO THROUGH EVERY DAY
- BUT IF IT WASN'T *HARD*, WE WOULD REMAIN COMPLACENT

Panel 6:
- AND EXPERIENCING THE FEELINGS OTHERS FEEL . . . IT'S SORT OF LIKE *WAKING UP*
- THAT'S AN ODD WAY TO SA--

Panel 7: (sleeping)

Panel 8:
- SO WHAT WAS ALL THAT YELLING ABOUT?
- YOU MEAN THAT ACTUALLY HAPPENED?
- WOULD YOU LIKE TO SEE MY GIANT BLUE GRYPHON FEATHER?

Panel 9:
- WHAT MAKES YOU THINK YOU'RE NOT "GOOD ENOUGH"?
- BECAUSE YOU'RE AWESOME, AND ALL I EVER DO IS SCREW UP . . .

Panel 10:
- MAXIE, SCREWING UP DOESN'T MEAN YOU'RE A SCREWUP
- WE *ALL* MAKE MISTAKES; WHY HOLD THEM AGAINST ONE ANOTHER?

Panel 11:
- GUESS WHO'S SLEEPING IN THE DOGHOUSE FOR THAT 'NORMAL' JAB, HONEY?
- WE DON'T EVEN LIVE TOGETHER!
- *WE'LL SEE ABOUT THAT!*

END!

Panel 12: (fox with tablet, "?")

Panel 13: (fox gesturing)

Panel 14: (fox with pot, steam)

Panel 15:
- UH, THE TABLET *YOU* GAVE ME SAYS "TOUCH ANYWHERE TO CONTINUE" AND IT'S NOT WORKING!

Panel 16: (fox at shelf)

Panel 17: (!)

Panel 18:
- WHAT ARE YOU DOING?!
- BEEP

Panel 19: (fox with tablet)

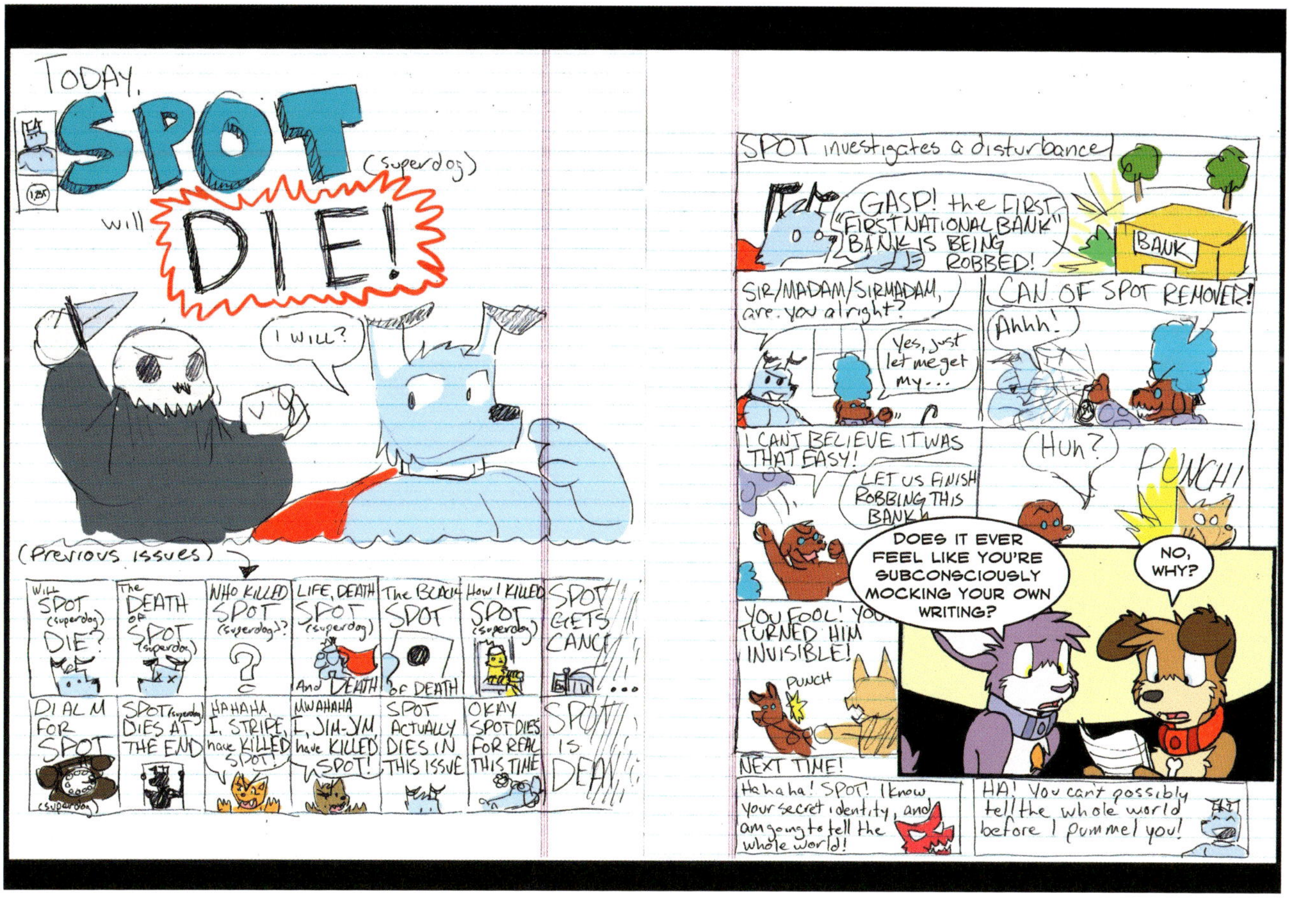
TODAY,
SPOT (superdog)
will DIE!
I WILL?
(Previous issues)
WILL SPOT (superdog) DIE?
The DEATH OF SPOT (superdog)
WHO KILLED SPOT (superdog)?
LIFE, DEATH SPOT (superdog) And DEATH
The BLACK SPOT of DEATH
How I KILLED SPOT (superdog)
SPOT GETS CANC...
DIAL M FOR SPOT (superdog)
SPOT (superdog) DIES AT THE END
HAHAHA, I, STRIPE, have KILLED SPOT!
MWAHAHA I, JIM-YM, have KILLED SPOT!
SPOT ACTUALLY DIES IN THIS ISSUE
OKAY SPOT DIES FOR REAL THIS TIME
SPOT IS DEAD
SPOT investigates a disturbance
GASP! the FIRST "FIRST NATIONAL BANK" BANK IS BEING ROBBED!
BANK
SIR/MADAM/SIRMADAM, are you alright?
Yes, just let me get my...
CAN OF SPOT REMOVER!
Ahhh!
I CAN'T BELIEVE IT WAS THAT EASY!
LET US FINISH ROBBING THIS BANK
Huh?
PUNCH!
DOES IT EVER FEEL LIKE YOU'RE SUBCONSCIOUSLY MOCKING YOUR OWN WRITING?
NO, WHY?
YOU FOOL! YOU TURNED HIM INVISIBLE!
PUNCH
NEXT TIME!
Hahaha! SPOT! I know your secret identity, and am going to tell the whole world!
HA! You can't possibly tell the whole world before I pummel you!

THE ADVENTURES OF (new) SPOT (superdog)
SPOT and the COST of BUSINESS!
BANK
SPOT, Your new movie has done gangbusters in theaters — both figuratively and literally!
Awesome!
PUNCHED
Of course, by "gangbusters" I mean really, really awful
What?? Didn't we sell twenty million tickets?!
Don't tell me you're going to blame inflation or Global Farming or something like that
Certainly not — the issue is that sales did not meet our entirely reasonable expectations
$$$
Consider, please, the highly economic flowchart
Principle: You must spend money to make money
THEREFORE to make gobs of money, you must spend gobs of money
= FLAWLESS SCHEME!
DON'T YOU THINK YOU'RE EDITORIALIZING A BIT MUCH?
A LITTLE, BUT THAT'S WHY PEOPLE MAKE COMICS, RIGHT?
And how much gobs was in your expectations?
Given that your previous movie cost 200 million to make and returned 800 million, this shows a trend of 4x returns
So given we wanted to make $4 billion...
YOU SPENT $1 BILLION ON MY MOVIE?? FOR WHAT??
Please! Our trends ALSO show we can't make money without a $300 million nude scene—
LATER...
RIP JOHN A. EXECUTIVE "So very dumb for a stupid guy"

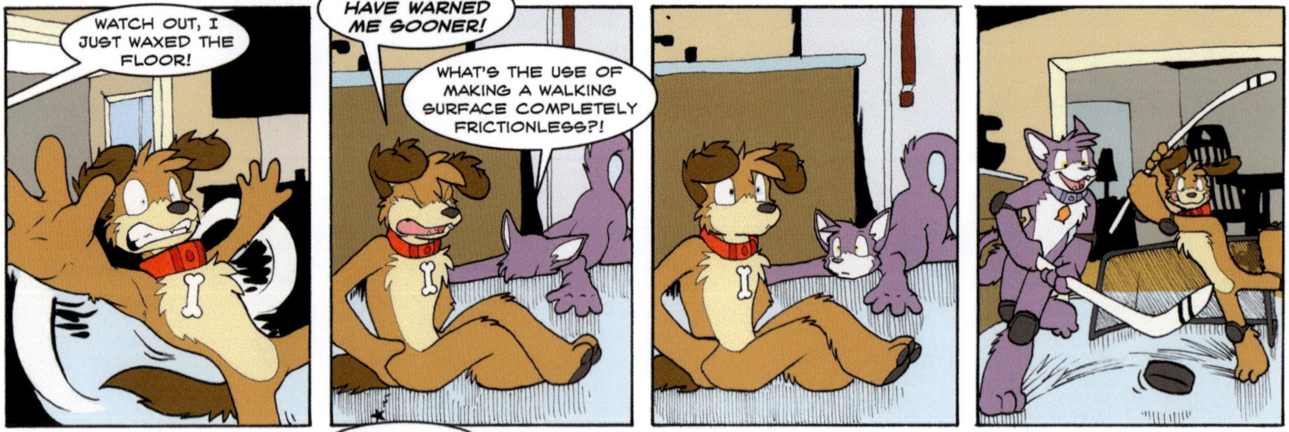
WATCH OUT, I JUST WAXED THE FLOOR!
YOU COULD HAVE WARNED ME SOONER!
WHAT'S THE USE OF MAKING A WALKING SURFACE COMPLETELY FRICTIONLESS?!

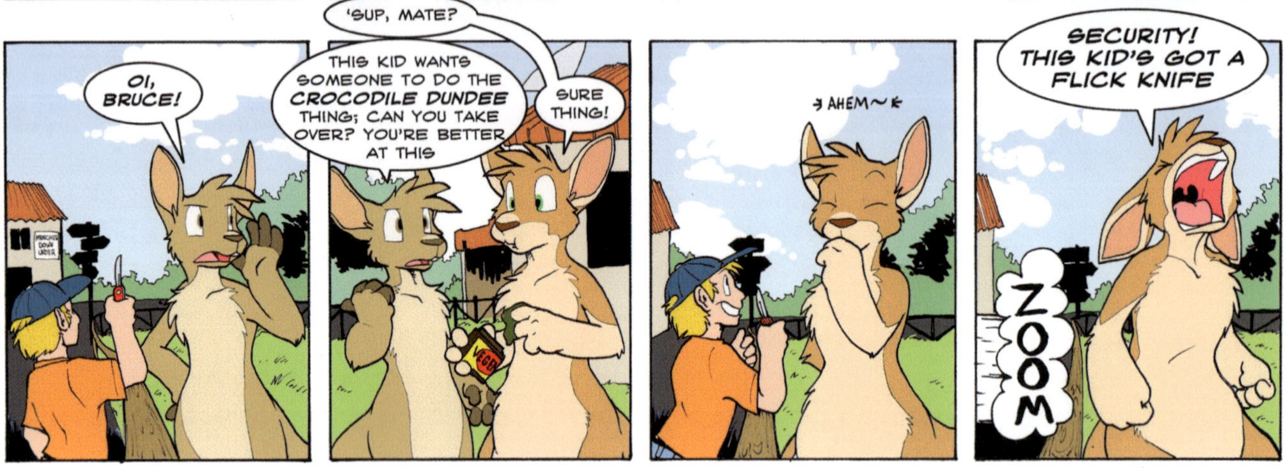
OI, BRUCE!
'SUP, MATE?
THIS KID WANTS SOMEONE TO DO THE CROCODILE DUNDEE THING; CAN YOU TAKE OVER? YOU'RE BETTER AT THIS
SURE THING!
AHEM~
SECURITY! THIS KID'S GOT A FLICK KNIFE
ZOOM

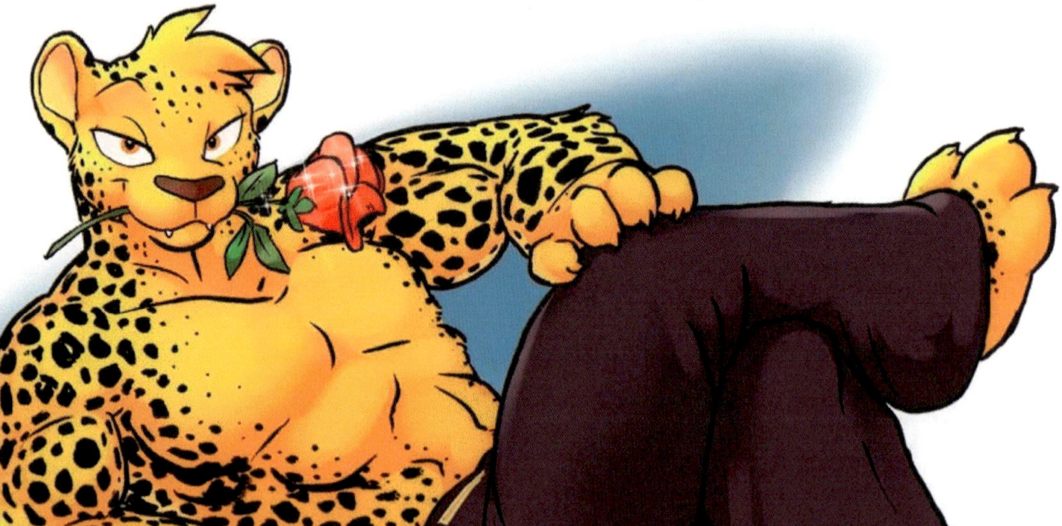

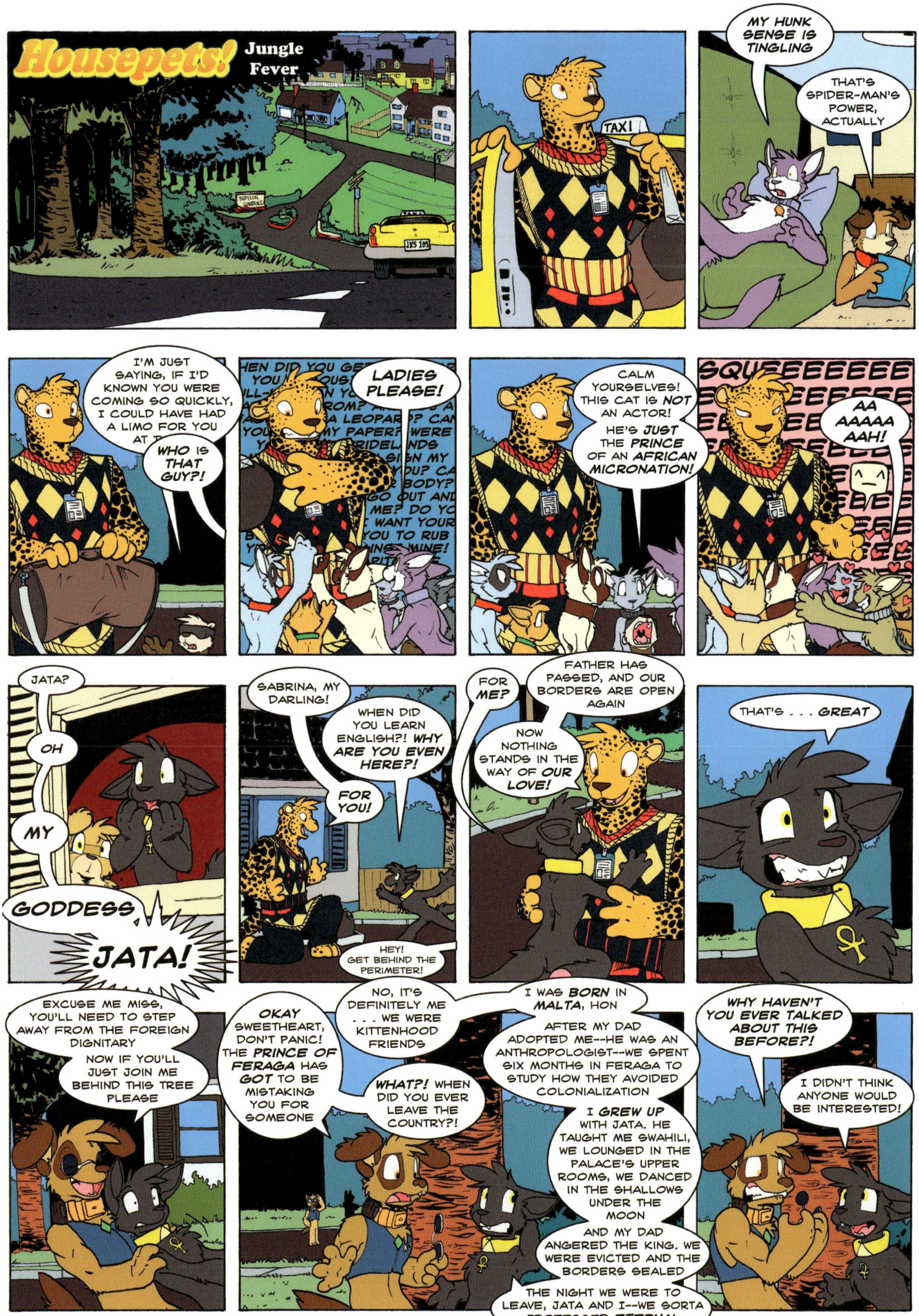

Housepets! Jungle Fever
TAXI
MY HUNK SENSE IS TINGLING
THAT'S SPIDER-MAN'S POWER, ACTUALLY
I'M JUST SAYING, IF I'D KNOWN YOU WERE COMING SO QUICKLY, I COULD HAVE HAD A LIMO FOR YOU AT T—
WHO IS THAT GUY?!
LADIES PLEASE!
CALM YOURSELVES! THIS CAT IS NOT AN ACTOR!
HE'S JUST THE PRINCE OF AN AFRICAN MICRONATION!
SQUEEEEEEEEEEEEE
AA AAAAA AAH!
JATA?
OH
MY
GODDESS,
JATA!
SABRINA, MY DARLING!
WHEN DID YOU LEARN ENGLISH?! WHY ARE YOU EVEN HERE?!
FOR YOU!
HEY! GET BEHIND THE PERIMETER!
FOR ME?
FATHER HAS PASSED, AND OUR BORDERS ARE OPEN AGAIN
NOW NOTHING STANDS IN THE WAY OF OUR LOVE!
THAT'S . . . GREAT
EXCUSE ME MISS, YOU'LL NEED TO STEP AWAY FROM THE FOREIGN DIGNITARY
NOW IF YOU'LL JUST JOIN ME BEHIND THIS TREE PLEASE
OKAY SWEETHEART, DON'T PANIC! THE PRINCE OF FERAGA HAS GOT TO BE MISTAKING YOU FOR SOMEONE
NO, IT'S DEFINITELY ME . . . WE WERE KITTENHOOD FRIENDS
WHAT?! WHEN DID YOU EVER LEAVE THE COUNTRY?!
I WAS BORN IN MALTA, HON
AFTER MY DAD ADOPTED ME--HE WAS AN ANTHROPOLOGIST--WE SPENT SIX MONTHS IN FERAGA TO STUDY HOW THEY AVOIDED COLONIALIZATION
I GREW UP WITH JATA. HE TAUGHT ME SWAHILI, WE LOUNGED IN THE PALACE'S UPPER ROOMS, WE DANCED IN THE SHALLOWS UNDER THE MOON
AND MY DAD ANGERED THE KING. WE WERE EVICTED AND THE BORDERS SEALED
THE NIGHT WE WERE TO LEAVE, JATA AND I--WE SORTA PROFESSED ETERNAL LOVE
WHY HAVEN'T YOU EVER TALKED ABOUT THIS BEFORE?!
I DIDN'T THINK ANYONE WOULD BE INTERESTED!

THE REASON I CALLED . . . I HAVE A REALLY, REALLY, REALLY REALLY REALLY REALLY REALLY REALLY BIG FAVOR TO ASK
. . . CAN YOU BE MY PRETEND BF? FOR LIKE, A WEEK?
WELL LOOKIE WHO COMES MEWLING BACK! IT SEEMS THE MITTEN IS ON THE OTHER KITTEN NOW!
I'LL TELL YOU WHAT, I'M FEELING GENEROUS, SO THIS WILL BE RELATIVELY CHEAP
OH, SIX POUNDS OF CATNIP IS GOOD TO START, AND YOU'LL HAVE TO TELL EVERYONE HOW ADORABLE I AM--IF WE ARE, AS YOU SAY, GOING TO MEET ROYALTY, I'LL NEED A NEW--
!
WHATEVER YOU TWO ARE PLANNING I'LL DO IT FOR FREE!
GYHK!
SEE YOU AT SIX, HON~
YES, MR. MILTON HIRED US--WE'RE CURRENTLY DETAILED AS YOUR BODYGUARDS
AH! NEAT!
HAVING GOTTEN ALONG FINE WITHOUT HUMANS, I BELIEVE IF ANIMALS ARE GOING TO BE HELP, IT'S TO OTHER ANIMALS
GREETINGS, ELDER! WHAT'S YOUR STATION HERE?
IS HE TRYING TO JUDGE MY CHARACTER BY MY FACE?
NO, UNCLE DEADEYE ALREADY DECIDED HE DOESN'T LIKE YOU
SO HE'S JUST SMOTHERING YOU
YOUR HIGHNESS, MISS D'ANGELO IS HERE AS YOU REQUESTED
MY THANKS, PALE HUMAN! YOU'RE A CREDIT TO YOUR SPECIES
GRUMBLE YESSUH
HEY BABE . . . YOU JUST CAUGHT ME COMING OUT OF THE SHOWER
YEAH, HEY JATA, I'M REALLY EXCITED FOR OUR DATE!
WE'RE GONNA HAVE SO MUCH TO CATCH UP ON!
PLUS, YOU NEED TO MEET MY BOYFRIEND, CONCORD!
THAT'S CUTE. I'M GOING TO GET DRESSED, SEE YOU OUT BY THE LIMO!
I'M OKAY WITH THIS ARRANGEMENT
GRAPE, THAT'S NOT REALLY AN OPTION--
I'M JUST MESSING AROUND! I KNOW I AIN'T GOT A SERIOUS SHOT AT A REAL-LIFE PRIDELANDS PRINCE!
BUT DOES MAX KNOW THAT?
MAXIE'S FINE! WHAT'S HE GOT TO WORRY ABOUT?
I'M NOT A PRAYING CAT, BUT I KNOW WHEN I REQUIRE THE ASSISTANCE OF A HIGHER POWER
I CANNOT GO ON LIVING IN A PERPETUAL SECOND PLACE! SO PLEASE, I BEG OF YOU . . .
CHISEL ME INTO A MIGHTY STONE GOD!
WANT YOU
GYM
PAIN DOES NOT HURT

AND SO!
. . . AND WELL, THAT'S HOW I MET CONCORD
EACH STORY YOU TELL IS BETTER THAN THE LAST! CONCORD HAS BEEN LUCKY TO HAVE YOU
HE DOESN'T SEEM TO OPEN HIS MOUTH TOO MUCH, DOES HE?
IT'S BETTER THAN DISCOVERING HOW MANY FEET CAN FIT IN THERE
I BEG YOUR PARDON, BUT I NEED TO VISIT, AS YOU PUT IT, THE SANDBOX
I JUST SAY THE TOILET, BUT HAVE FUN ANYHOW
SABRINA! WE HAVE A BIG PROBLEM!
I'M HANDLING IT, FIDEY. JATA ALREADY KNOWS I'M ATTACHED AND SEEMS FINE WITH IT
IT'S NOT THAT! I WAS TALKING WITH THE K-9S AND--
. . . IS THERE SOMETHING ELSE YOU NEED TO TELL ME?
OH HUSH, IT'S FUN
HE'S COMING BACK, UNDER THE TABLE
GYKH!
WELL MY DEAR, THIS HAS BEEN AN INFORMATIVE EVENING
BUT NOW IT'S TIME TO LAY THINGS ASIDE AND FOCUS ON OUR FUTURE
OKAY WAIT, DIDN'T YOU GET THE HINT? I'M IN LOVE WITH--ER--CONCORD!
YES BUT WE PLEDGED OUR LOVE! THAT'S A LEGAL OBLIGATION!
I WAS SIX MONTHS OLD!
AND I WAS EIGHTEEN MONTHS! AH, THE VICISSITUDES OF YOUNG LOVE
THAT CAN'T BE AN ENFORCABLE CONTRACT!
IT WOULDN'T FOR A US CITIZEN, WHICH YOU ARE NOT
OH, RIGHT
PET
AND REALLY, WOULDN'T IT BE BETTER TO LIVE IN A LAND WHERE YOU HAD POLITICAL RESPECT?
HEY! WHAT IF SHE DOESN'T WANT TO GO BACK TO AFRICA?
I SUPPOSE WE COULD SETTLE THIS IN TRUE FERAGA TRADITION! THE SUITORS WILL FACE ONE ANOTHER IN--
--TRIAL BY COMBAT!
!
HA HA HA! HE PASSED OUT FROM SHEER FRIGHT!
YEAH, WE'LL GO WITH THAT

YOU DON'T HAVE TO WORRY, I DON'T EXPECT YOU TO STAY IN AFRICA THE REST OF YOUR LIFE--
PHEW
--THE MARRIAGE IS THE IMPORTANT PART, AFTER ALL
MARRIAGE?! JATA SERIOUSLY, WHY ARE YOU DOING THIS!?
IT IS FOR BOTH OF OUR MUTUAL BENEFITS--FOR MY COUNTRY AND YOUR OWN!
THE GOOD OF THE COUNTRY?! WHO TOLD YOU THAT?
HEY JEEVES, WHILE YOU'RE OUT CAN YOU GRAB SOME ALOE LOTION?
FOR SOME REASON MY EARS ARE BURNING
OH DON'T BE SO DRAMATIC MY LOVE; MARRIAGE IS JUST SILLY WORDS
SEE YOU IN THE LIMO SWEETHEART~
YOU COULDN'T HAVE BEEN FIVE MINUTES EARLIER?
I TRIED!
BAK
. . . THAT'S WHAT I HEARD, ANYWAY. I DON'T UNDERSTAND, THOUGH, I THOUGHT PETS COULDN'T DO LEGAL ANYTHING WITHOUT OWNER CONSENT
THAT'S NOT HOW IT WORKS IN FERAGA
WHAT DO YOU MEAN?
IT WAS ONE OF THE FIRST THINGS MY DAD LEARNED
FERAGA WAS SO STAUNCHLY AGAINST THE PRACTICE OF SLAVERY, I COULDN'T BE A "PET" INSIDE THEIR BORDERS
I WAS A FREE CITIZEN THE WHOLE TIME
WAIT, THEY HATE THE CONCEPT OF BEING OWNED, BUT SEE NOTHING WRONG WITH A SHOTGUN WEDDING?!
I THINK, BEFORE THEY LET YOU INTO POLITICS, YOU NEED TO FIRST PROVE YOU'RE A MASSIVE HYPOCRITE
THE ARRANGEMENT WASN'T MY SUGGESTION, IT WAS JUST BENEFICIAL TO ME
I GET LEGAL PRECEDENT, FERAGA GETS SOME MODERN INDUSTRY
YOU FUZZY SNAKE! IF THIS IS ABOUT LEGALITY, I DEMAND A STAY OF THE WEDDING UNTIL THE LAW HAS BEEN REVIEWED!
YEAH, ABOUT THAT
HAVE YOU MET MY FRIEND, JUDGE JANSSEN OF THE HAGUE?
YOU SAID YOU DIDN'T WANT TO BE EVIL!
I SAID I DIDN'T WANT TO BE A MONSTER
FINE DIFFERENCE THERE

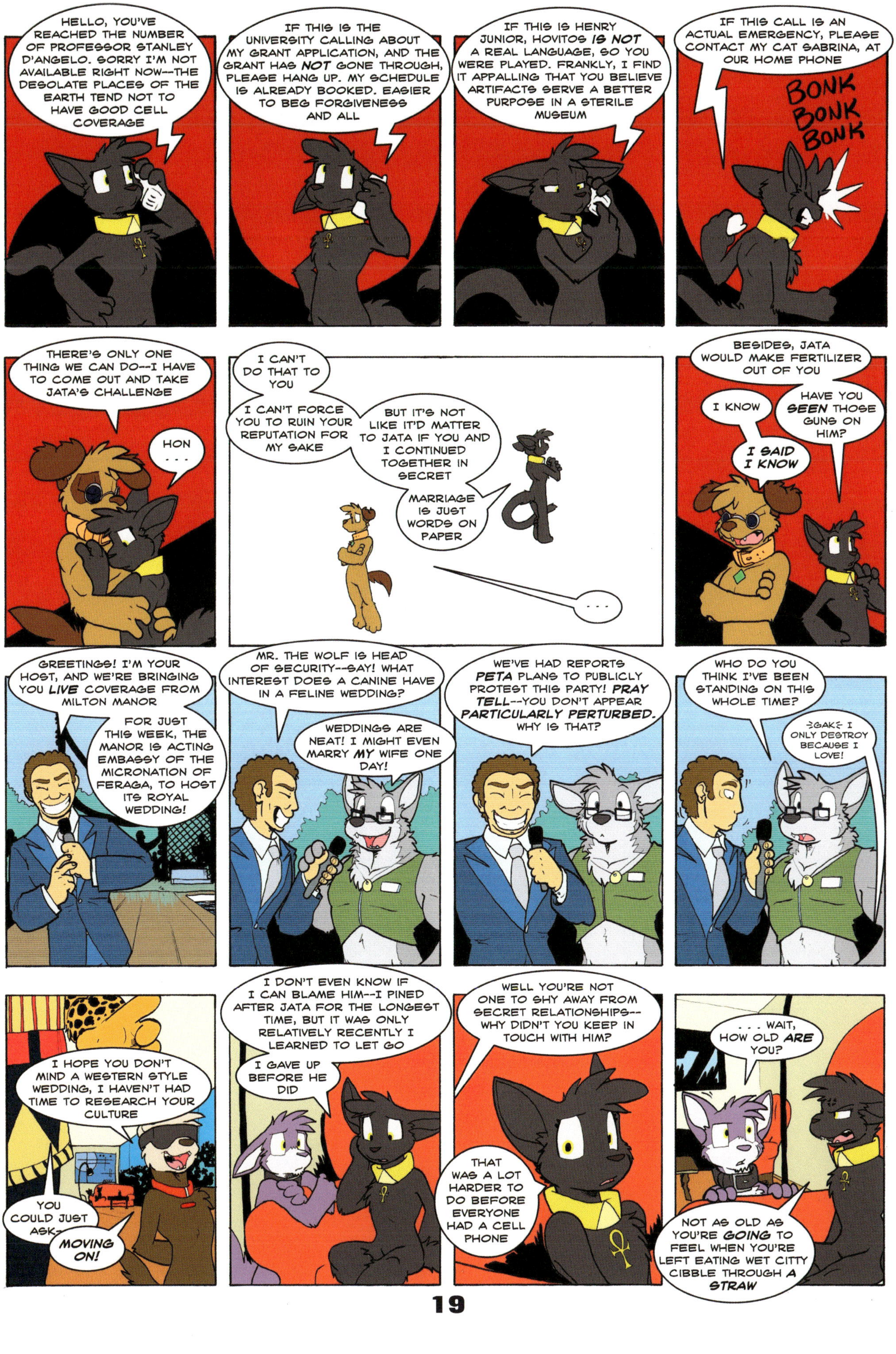
HELLO, YOU'VE REACHED THE NUMBER OF PROFESSOR STANLEY D'ANGELO. SORRY I'M NOT AVAILABLE RIGHT NOW--THE DESOLATE PLACES OF THE EARTH TEND NOT TO HAVE GOOD CELL COVERAGE
IF THIS IS THE UNIVERSITY CALLING ABOUT MY GRANT APPLICATION, AND THE GRANT HAS NOT GONE THROUGH, PLEASE HANG UP. MY SCHEDULE IS ALREADY BOOKED. EASIER TO BEG FORGIVENESS AND ALL
IF THIS IS HENRY JUNIOR, HOVITOS IS NOT A REAL LANGUAGE, SO YOU WERE PLAYED. FRANKLY, I FIND IT APPALLING THAT YOU BELIEVE ARTIFACTS SERVE A BETTER PURPOSE IN A STERILE MUSEUM
IF THIS CALL IS AN ACTUAL EMERGENCY, PLEASE CONTACT MY CAT SABRINA, AT OUR HOME PHONE
BONK BONK BONK
THERE'S ONLY ONE THING WE CAN DO--I HAVE TO COME OUT AND TAKE JATA'S CHALLENGE
HON . . .
I CAN'T DO THAT TO YOU
I CAN'T FORCE YOU TO RUIN YOUR REPUTATION FOR MY SAKE
BUT IT'S NOT LIKE IT'D MATTER TO JATA IF YOU AND I CONTINUED TOGETHER IN SECRET
MARRIAGE IS JUST WORDS ON PAPER
. . .
BESIDES, JATA WOULD MAKE FERTILIZER OUT OF YOU
I KNOW
HAVE YOU SEEN THOSE GUNS ON HIM?
I SAID I KNOW
GREETINGS! I'M YOUR HOST, AND WE'RE BRINGING YOU LIVE COVERAGE FROM MILTON MANOR
FOR JUST THIS WEEK, THE MANOR IS ACTING EMBASSY OF THE MICRONATION OF FERAGA, TO HOST ITS ROYAL WEDDING!
MR. THE WOLF IS HEAD OF SECURITY--SAY! WHAT INTEREST DOES A CANINE HAVE IN A FELINE WEDDING?
WEDDINGS ARE NEAT! I MIGHT EVEN MARRY MY WIFE ONE DAY!
WE'VE HAD REPORTS PETA PLANS TO PUBLICLY PROTEST THIS PARTY! PRAY TELL--YOU DON'T APPEAR PARTICULARLY PERTURBED. WHY IS THAT?
WHO DO YOU THINK I'VE BEEN STANDING ON THIS WHOLE TIME?
GAK I ONLY DESTROY BECAUSE I LOVE!
I HOPE YOU DON'T MIND A WESTERN STYLE WEDDING, I HAVEN'T HAD TIME TO RESEARCH YOUR CULTURE
YOU COULD JUST ASK—
MOVING ON!
I DON'T EVEN KNOW IF I CAN BLAME HIM--I PINED AFTER JATA FOR THE LONGEST TIME, BUT IT WAS ONLY RELATIVELY RECENTLY I LEARNED TO LET GO
I GAVE UP BEFORE HE DID
WELL YOU'RE NOT ONE TO SHY AWAY FROM SECRET RELATIONSHIPS--WHY DIDN'T YOU KEEP IN TOUCH WITH HIM?
THAT WAS A LOT HARDER TO DO BEFORE EVERYONE HAD A CELL PHONE
. . . WAIT, HOW OLD ARE YOU?
NOT AS OLD AS YOU'RE GOING TO FEEL WHEN YOU'RE LEFT EATING WET CITTY CIBBLE THROUGH A STRAW

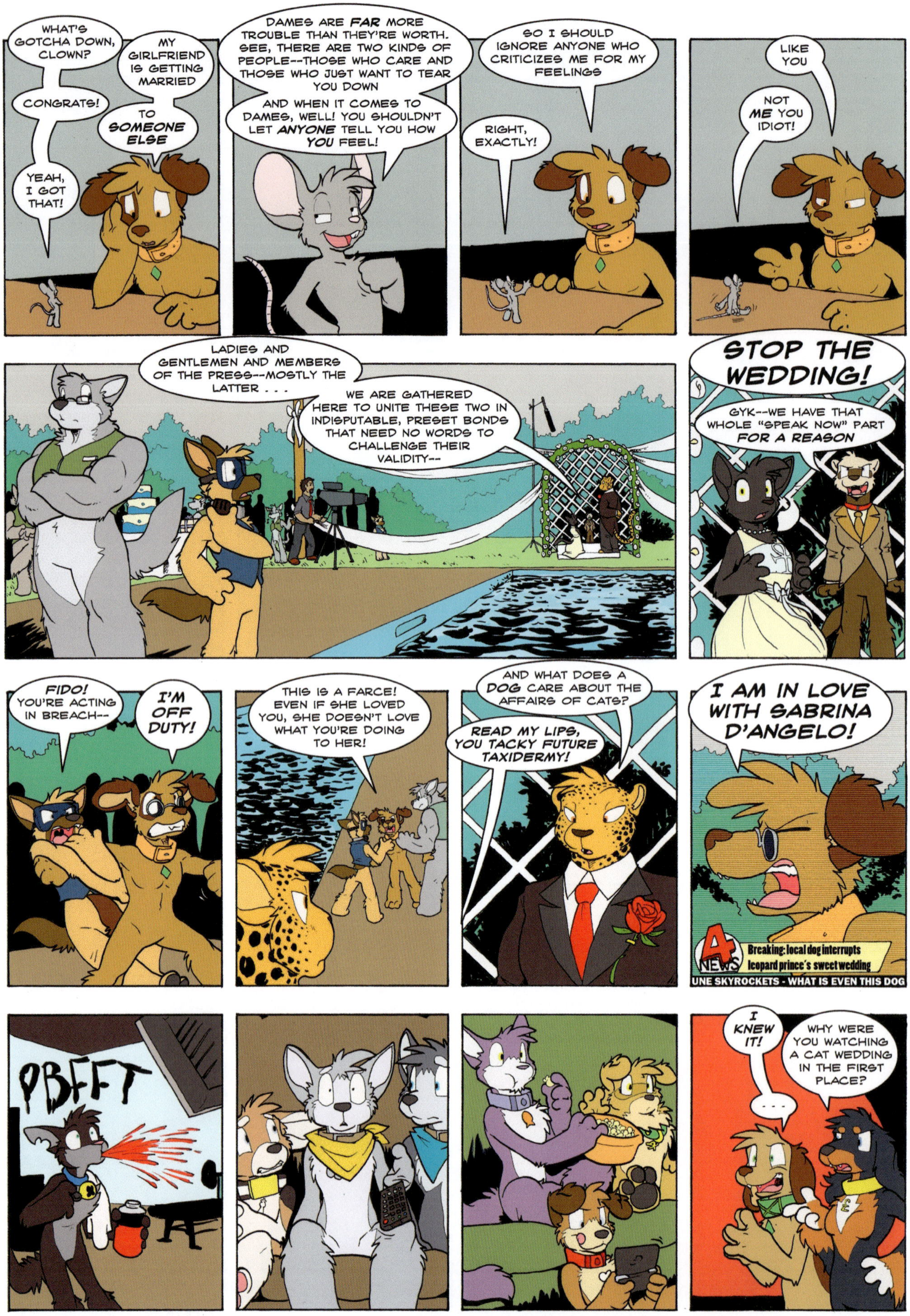

WHAT'S GOTCHA DOWN, CLOWN?
MY GIRLFRIEND IS GETTING MARRIED
CONGRATS!
TO *SOMEONE ELSE*
YEAH, I GOT THAT!
DAMES ARE *FAR* MORE TROUBLE THAN THEY'RE WORTH. SEE, THERE ARE TWO KINDS OF PEOPLE--THOSE WHO CARE AND THOSE WHO JUST WANT TO TEAR YOU DOWN
AND WHEN IT COMES TO DAMES, WELL! YOU SHOULDN'T LET *ANYONE* TELL YOU HOW *YOU* FEEL!
SO I SHOULD IGNORE ANYONE WHO CRITICIZES ME FOR MY FEELINGS
RIGHT, EXACTLY!
LIKE YOU
NOT *ME* YOU IDIOT!
LADIES AND GENTLEMEN AND MEMBERS OF THE PRESS--MOSTLY THE LATTER . . .
WE ARE GATHERED HERE TO UNITE THESE TWO IN INDISPUTABLE, PRESET BONDS THAT NEED NO WORDS TO CHALLENGE THEIR VALIDITY--
STOP THE WEDDING!
GYK--WE HAVE THAT WHOLE "SPEAK NOW" PART *FOR A REASON*
FIDO! YOU'RE ACTING IN BREACH--
I'M OFF DUTY!
THIS IS A FARCE! EVEN IF SHE LOVED YOU, SHE DOESN'T LOVE WHAT YOU'RE DOING TO HER!
AND WHAT DOES A *DOG* CARE ABOUT THE AFFAIRS OF CATS?
READ MY LIPS, YOU TACKY FUTURE TAXIDERMY!
I AM IN LOVE WITH SABRINA D'ANGELO!
4 NEWS
Breaking: local dog interrupts leopard prince's sweet wedding
UNE SKYROCKETS - WHAT IS EVEN THIS DOG
PBFFT
I KNEW IT!
. . .
WHY WERE YOU WATCHING A CAT WEDDING IN THE FIRST PLACE?

WHAT IS THIS . . . A JOKE? IS THIS YOUR AMERICAN SENSE OF HUMOR?
. . . BECAUSE I HAVE TO SAY, IT IS PRETTY FUNNY!
IT'S TRUE, JATA
FIDO IS MY REAL BOYFRIEND
I SEE . . .
THIS "CONCORD" DECEPTION WAS TO SAVE FACE
IT FALLS TO ME, THEN, TO SAVE YOU FROM THIS SHAME!
THE TRIAL BY COMBAT BEGINS NOW!
DOG! PREPARE YOURSELF . . . TO LOSE!
YOU SEE, I CAN MAKE A JOKE TOO!
CATCH! (?)
!
GOON SQUAD!
WHERE IS MY GOON SQUAD?!
HELLO THERE!
FIDO TOLD ME YOU GUYS LIKE TO PLAY CORNHOLE?
!
THIS HAS GONE FAR ENOUGH!
WHO DARES?!
YOU WOULD USE YOUR LAWS TO SEPARATE TWO WHO LOVE EACH OTHER?
TELL ME, LEOPARD, DO SUCH LAWS LET THE OPPONENT SELECT . . .
A CHAMPION?
LAWLESS FERALS!
THE PRINCE OF FERAGA TAKES ON ALL COMERS!
HEY! YOU'RE NOT RISKING AN INTERNATIONAL INCIDENT UNDER MY WATCH! EVERYONE IS UNDER ARREST!
OF COURSE THIS FINALLY HAPPENS AFTER OUR EXCLUSIVE CONTRACT LAPSES!

JATA PLEASE! YOU DON'T HAVE TO DO THIS! ***WHAT DO YOU HAVE TO PROVE?!***
HUH
I WAS SURE IT'D BE A LAKE
20'

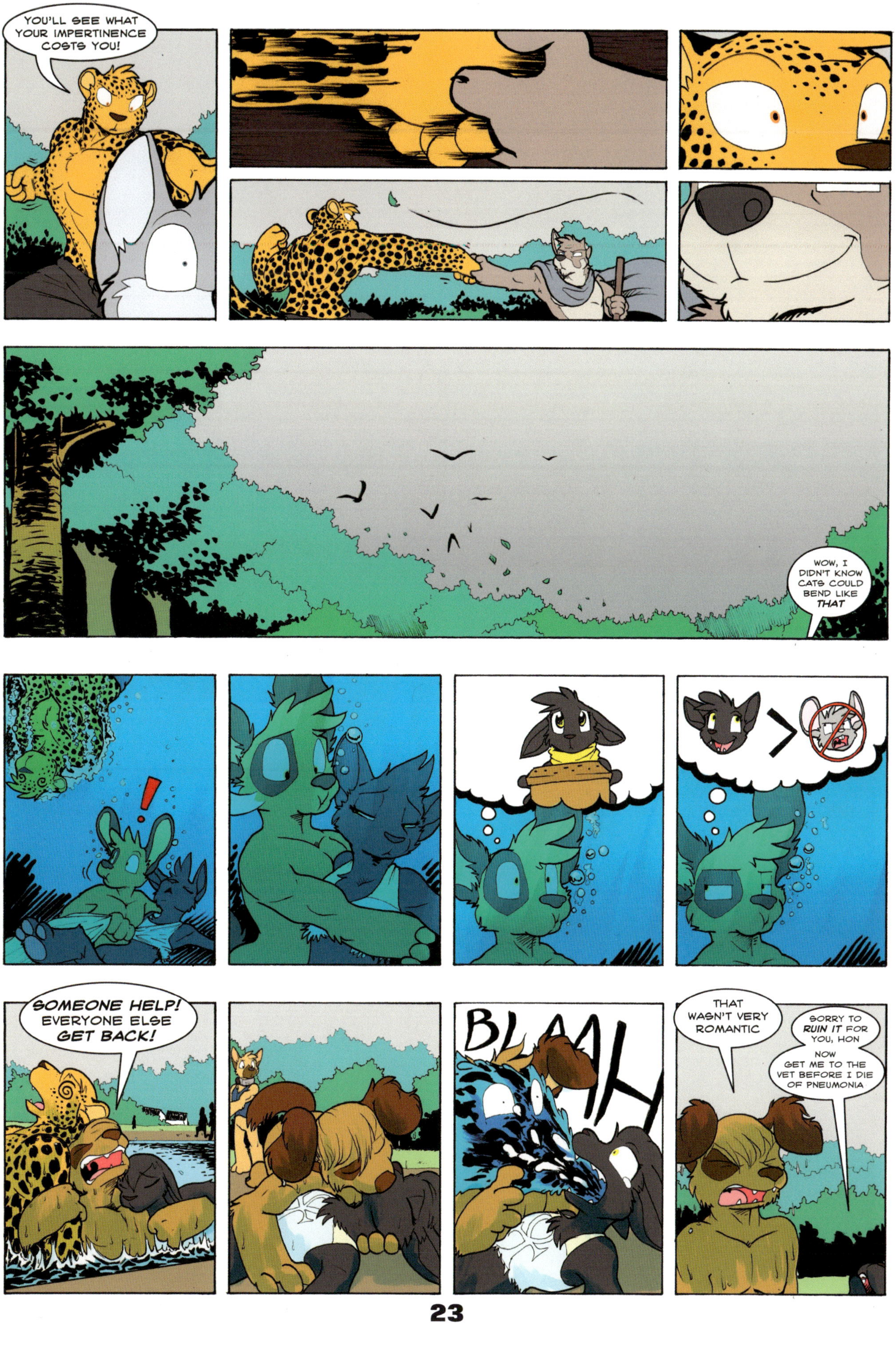
YOU'LL SEE WHAT YOUR IMPERTINENCE COSTS YOU!
WOW, I DIDN'T KNOW CATS COULD BEND LIKE THAT
!
SOMEONE HELP! EVERYONE ELSE GET BACK!
BLAAH
THAT WASN'T VERY ROMANTIC
SORRY TO RUIN IT FOR YOU, HON
NOW GET ME TO THE VET BEFORE I DIE OF PNEUMONIA

-SIGH-
PUNCH
CAN YOU IMAGINE THE PUBLICITY THIS IS GOING TO GENERATE?
I KNOW, RIGHT?!
. . . AND SINCE THE MILTON MANOR WAS A FERAGA EMBASSY, ALL ACTIONS ON THEIR TERRITORY WOULD, TECHNICALLY, FALL UNDER FERAGA LAW
THE INVOLVEMENT OF US CITIZENS MAY BE AN ISSUE, BUT THAT DOESN'T INCLUDE ANY OF US
SO, BEFORE YOU'RE SHUFFLED OFF ON ADMINISTRATIVE LEAVE, CAN YOU EXPLAIN JUST WHAT WAS THAT STUNT YOU PULLED?
ERM . . .
IT'S ALL TRUE, SIR. I AM IN LOVE WITH A CAT AND I CAN'T TOLERATE THE CHARADE ANY LONGER
NO MATTER WHAT ANYONE MIGHT SAY, I REFUSE TO SURRENDER ON THIS MATTER
THAT'S GOOD!
GOOD?!
I'VE HAD MY EYE ON YOU FOR A WHILE. YOUR SUSPICIOUS BEHAVIOR WORRIED ME
I THOUGHT YOU WERE PARTICIPATING IN SOMETHING UNDERHANDED--OR WORSE, ILLEGAL
WHO YOU DECIDE TO SNUGGLE WITH AFTER HOURS IS NONE OF THE DEPARTMENT'S BUSINESS NOR CONCERN
BUT YOUR CHOICE TO NOT WARN YOUR SQUADMATES OF YOUR ACTIONS IS CONCERNING. WE COULD HAVE AVOIDED A LOT OF BRUISES AND PAPERWORK
SEE YOU IN THREE WEEKS
SO . . . DO YOU LET HER CHASE YOU? IS THAT HOW THAT WORKS?
HA-HA! I FEEL LIKE A TOTALLY NEW CAT! SCRAWNY NO LONGER!
UH, YOU ONLY MADE IT TO HALF A REP--
JEALOUSY WILL NOT SERVE YOU!
AFTER
BEFORE
SAY THERE HOT STUFF, I'M NEW IN TOWN, YOU WOULDN'T HAPPEN TO KNOW WHICH WAY TO THE BEACH?
POSE!
OH MAXIE, I'D THINK YOU WERE PATHETIC IF YOU WEREN'T SO ADORABLE
CAREFUL BABE, GENEVA DECLARED POSESSION OF THESE GUNS A WAR CRIME

LET THE RECORD SHOW, BY A VOTE OF 4-1 . . . FIDO BYRON IS NO LONGER A MEMBER OF THIS COUNCIL
WE'LL BE HOLDING NEW ELECTIONS SOON, WON'T WE DUTCHIE-POO?
I SWEAR TO DOG I'LL DUMP YOUR TAIL IF YOU KEEP CALLING ME THAT
HOW'D IT TURN OUT?
I ABSTAINED. IT WOULDN'T HAVE MATTERED
I DON'T KNOW WHAT TO DO! THE WORLD SEEMS TO WORK IN ABSOLUTES, THEN IT TURNS OUT YOU'RE OLD FRIENDS WITH "THE WRONG SIDE"!
HAVE I BEEN WRONG ALL THIS TIME?! HOW CAN I EVEN BE SURE!?
I GUESS . . . ARE YOU MORE UPSET HE'S A CAT-LOVER, OR THAT HE KEPT IT A SECRET FROM YOU?
OH I'M LIVID HE KEPT THIS FROM ME!
. . . BUT I DON'T THINK I COULD BLAME HIM . . .
WELL, THAT'S SOMEWHAT COMFORTING
WHAT'S THAT SUPPOSED TO MEAN?!
I KNOW WE DIDN'T WORK OUT, BUT THAT DOESN'T MEAN WE HAVE TO HAVE BAD BLOOD!
MAYBE I COULD COME VISIT SOMETIME!
THAT WAS CLOSE
YOU TOLD ME THE FRIENDZONE WAS A MYTH!
NOW THAT I'M OUT OF THE BAG, YOU THINK THINGS WILL BE BETTER?
OH THEY WILL . . . JUST BEING ABLE TO SAY I LOVE YOU MAKES BURDENS RISE
OH NO! THE MATE OF THE LION-DUKE DISCOVERED I FLIRTED WITH HIM, AND SHE'S COMING HERE FOR REVENGE!
JUUUUST KIDDING!
LIFTED BURDENS ASIDE, WE CAN'T DISCOUNT THE FACT YOU UTTERLY TERRIFY ME
END!

Panel 1:
- "THIS WAS HIS IDEA"
- "OH NO YOU DON'T! THIS WAS *MY* IDEA!"

SPOT (superdog)

P.B.S. Comics — NOT A THREAT

When get-well cards aren't enough!

SPOT (superdog) is **SICK!**

"I didn't know you could GET sick!"

"Not ordinarily... but this is a foul disease from planet Orphan!"

"It's exactly like your earth flu, except a thousand times worse... and a thousand times more awesome!"

107°

"How's that?"

"Orphan flu causes hallucinations... that come to life!"

BOOM!

"Gasp! My archnemesis The Cyborg!"

"THAT'S RIGHT SPOT (superdog) I heard you were orphan-sick and came to give my condolences..."

"Now — DON'T THINK ABOUT ME HAVING AN INVINCIBLE ROBO-HORNET ARMY!"

POOF

"No! Must fight — too... weak...!"

JAB!

"Robo poison! It... ALSO causes hallucinations! What will— what... will..."

BOOM! (WOOOOOOO)

"Zzz... Yeah that's how it is... I'm superdog, awesome even when I'm sick... zzz"

Next time... SALUTING THE COMMIE FLAG?!

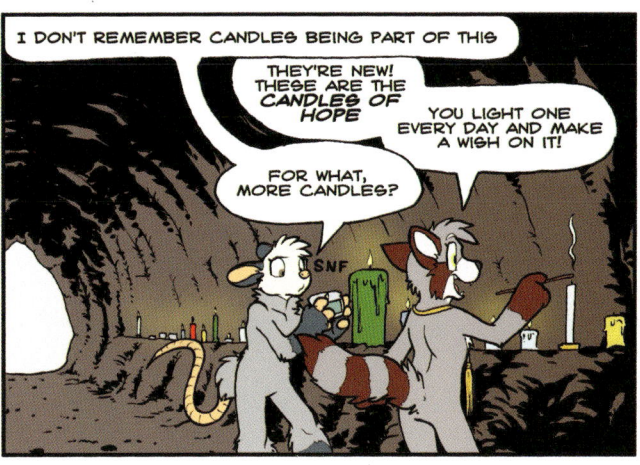

Housepets!
Yes, Jessica, There Is An Opener Of Ways

Panel 1: MERRY OPENERMAS JESS! / AUGH! INK! / BAM / TO THINK I USED TO BE HAPPIER AFTER THE BIRDS LEFT / IT SEEMS SO LONG AGO

Panel 2: WAIT, ISN'T OPENERMAS IN LIKE, THREE WEEKS? / IT HELPS YOU GET IN THE OPENERMAS SPIRIT! IT'S A TIME TO *OPEN* YOUR HEART--REALIZE THINGS WE CAN'T SEE AFFECT US EVERY DAY!

Panel 3: I AGREE! FROSTBITE, FOR INSTANCE / THAT'S THE SPIRIT!

Panel 4: I DON'T REMEMBER CANDLES BEING PART OF THIS / THEY'RE NEW! THESE ARE THE CANDLES OF HOPE / YOU LIGHT ONE EVERY DAY AND MAKE A WISH ON IT! / FOR WHAT, MORE CANDLES?

Panel 5: ACTUALLY, TODAY... =SIGH= MY SON CONTRACTED A FEVER LAST NIGHT / INK, UNDERSTAND YOU HAVE MY DEEPEST SYMPATHIES / BUT INSTEAD OF WISHING FOR MIRACLES, WOULDN'T YOUR SON APPRECIATE, OH, I DON'T KNOW, *SOME PENICILLIN?!*

Panel 6: I'M NOT AN *IDIOT*, JESS / THE WISH IS BECAUSE *FALSTAFF AND TRUCK* WERE THE ONES WHO WENT TO FETCH IT / OKAY, PERHAPS A TOUCH OF OPTIMISM *IS* NEEDED

Panel 7: I KNOW WE FACE TRYING TIMES, BUT WE CAN ONLY HOPE THE OPENER WILL ANSWER US / MOM SAYS I'M GONNA BE AN ANGEL!

Panel 8: OH TUM, YOUR TENACITY IS INSPIRING, BUT ANGELS ARE JUST A COMFORTING LIE, SWEETIE / JESSICA!

Panel 9: WELL IT'S TRUE! / I *GET* THAT YOU DON'T BELIEVE IN THE OPENER BUT CAN'T YOU DO SOMETHING OTHER THAN CRITICIZE US?! / FINE! I'LL GO DO SOMETHING USEFUL!

Panel 10: ...END THIS CHARADE! THE OPENER'S GONNA GET A PIECE OF MY MIND! / HE MIGHT NOT APPRECIATE THAT! HE'S VEGETARIAN!

Panel 11: STUPID WINTER. IF *I* WAS THE OPENER OF WAYS I'D BE AN IRRATIONAL FIGMENT WHEN IT WAS EASIER TO WALK...

Panel 12: ANYONE HOME? CAN YOU TELL ME HOW TO GET, HOW TO GET TO "BABYLON GARDENS"? / KNOCK KNOCK

Panel 13: EHEHEHEHE! TO GET TO THE OPENER'S STREET, I'LL EXPLAIN IT IN ANAPEST FEET! AT THE HILLTOP TURN RIGHT AND JUST FOLLOW THE LIGHT-- WARMER HEARTS THAN YOUR OWN WILL YOU MEET!

Panel 14: I DON'T MIND THE FORCED POETRY BUT I COULD DO WITHOUT THE UNSOLICITED MORALIZING / *YOU* PLED TO BE LED. GO SOAK YOUR HEAD

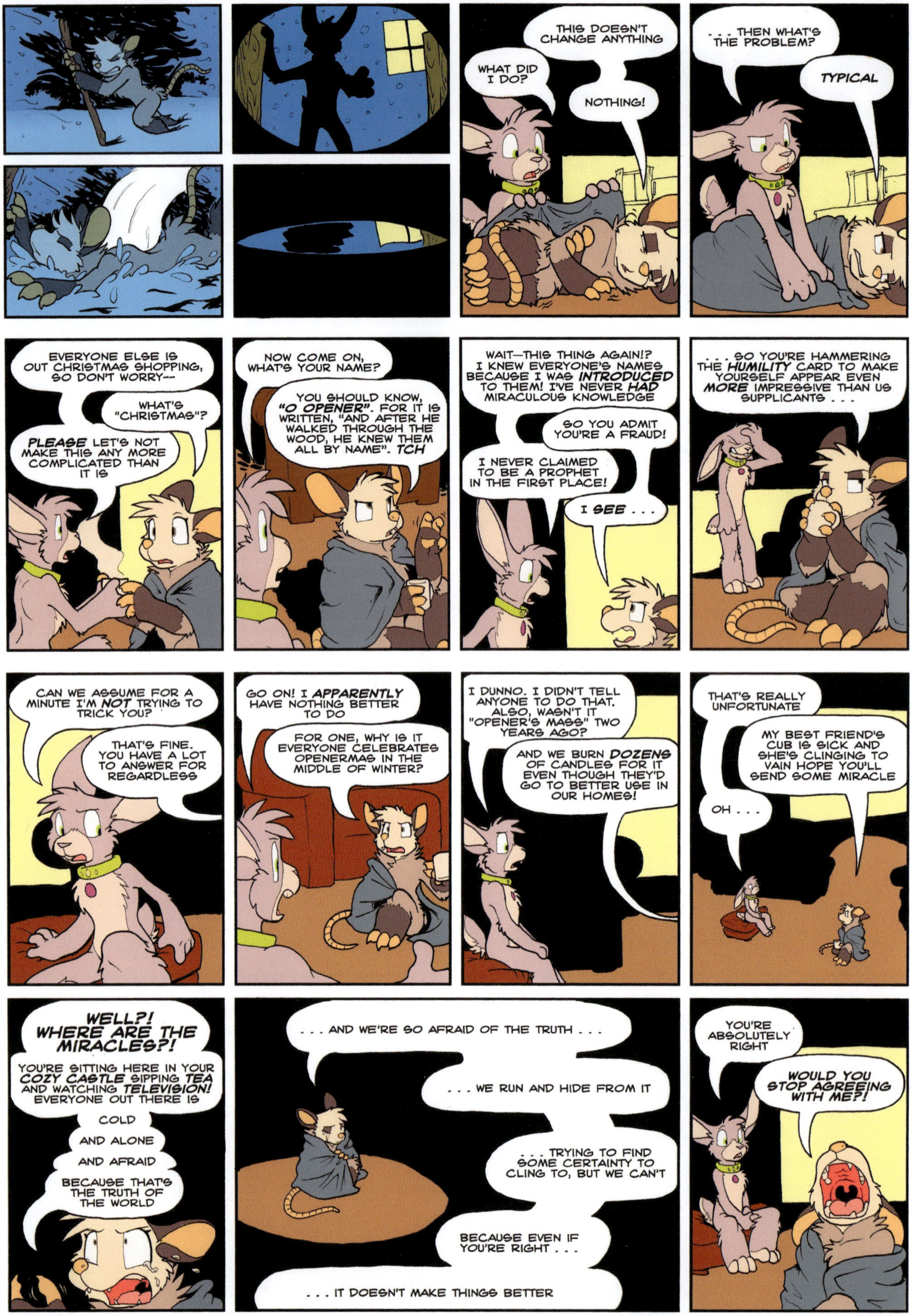
WHAT DID I DO?
THIS DOESN'T CHANGE ANYTHING
NOTHING!
. . . THEN WHAT'S THE PROBLEM?
TYPICAL
EVERYONE ELSE IS OUT CHRISTMAS SHOPPING, SO DON'T WORRY--
WHAT'S "CHRISTMAS"?
PLEASE LET'S NOT MAKE THIS ANY MORE COMPLICATED THAN IT IS
NOW COME ON, WHAT'S YOUR NAME?
YOU SHOULD KNOW, "O OPENER". FOR IT IS WRITTEN, "AND AFTER HE WALKED THROUGH THE WOOD, HE KNEW THEM ALL BY NAME". TCH
WAIT—THIS THING AGAIN!? I KNEW EVERYONE'S NAMES BECAUSE I WAS INTRODUCED TO THEM! I'VE NEVER HAD MIRACULOUS KNOWLEDGE
SO YOU ADMIT YOU'RE A FRAUD!
I NEVER CLAIMED TO BE A PROPHET IN THE FIRST PLACE!
I SEE . . .
. . . SO YOU'RE HAMMERING THE HUMILITY CARD TO MAKE YOURSELF APPEAR EVEN MORE IMPRESSIVE THAN US SUPPLICANTS . . .
CAN WE ASSUME FOR A MINUTE I'M NOT TRYING TO TRICK YOU?
THAT'S FINE. YOU HAVE A LOT TO ANSWER FOR REGARDLESS
GO ON! I APPARENTLY HAVE NOTHING BETTER TO DO
FOR ONE, WHY IS IT EVERYONE CELEBRATES OPENERMAS IN THE MIDDLE OF WINTER?
I DUNNO. I DIDN'T TELL ANYONE TO DO THAT. ALSO, WASN'T IT "OPENER'S MASS" TWO YEARS AGO?
AND WE BURN DOZENS OF CANDLES FOR IT EVEN THOUGH THEY'D GO TO BETTER USE IN OUR HOMES!
THAT'S REALLY UNFORTUNATE
MY BEST FRIEND'S CUB IS SICK AND SHE'S CLINGING TO VAIN HOPE YOU'LL SEND SOME MIRACLE
OH . . .
WELL?! WHERE ARE THE MIRACLES?!
YOU'RE SITTING HERE IN YOUR COZY CASTLE SIPPING TEA AND WATCHING TELEVISION! EVERYONE OUT THERE IS
COLD
AND ALONE
AND AFRAID
BECAUSE THAT'S THE TRUTH OF THE WORLD
. . . AND WE'RE SO AFRAID OF THE TRUTH . . .
. . . WE RUN AND HIDE FROM IT
. . . TRYING TO FIND SOME CERTAINTY TO CLING TO, BUT WE CAN'T
BECAUSE EVEN IF YOU'RE RIGHT . . .
. . . IT DOESN'T MAKE THINGS BETTER
YOU'RE ABSOLUTELY RIGHT
WOULD YOU STOP AGREEING WITH ME?!

I DON'T CARE IF YOU THINK I HAVE AN ULTERIOR MOTIVE. WE HAVE PLENTY OF STUFF WE NEVER USE, SO, TAKE THIS AND DO WHATEVER YOU THINK IS RIGHT
≈SIGH≈ . . . OKAY
ISN'T ASPIRIN JUST WILLOW BARK? WE *HAVE* THAT
IT'S HIGHLY CONCENTRATED
THAT'S JUST ANOTHER WORD FOR "POISONOUS"
I PRINTED OUT A FIELD GUIDE FOR EMERGENCY FERAL VETERINARY MEDICINE. ***PLEASE*** MAKE SURE IT DOESN'T END UP AS SCRIPTURE
THIS IS STUPID, HOW AM I SUPPOSED TO CARRY ALL THIS?
YOU JUST HAVE AN ANSWER FOR EVERYTHING, DON'T YOU?
GALLON FREEZER BAGS
DON'T WORRY, TUM! I'VE RETURNED WITH--
--MEDICINE
OH HEY JESS, TRUCK DID MAKE IT BACK AFTER ALL!
HEY
ANIMAL CONTROL PICKED UP FALS FOR RELOCATION AGAIN, SO, I DUNNO WHEN HE'LL BE BACK
OKAY
. . . HERE
JESS WAIT!
THANK YOU FOR THIS
WHY? I DIDN'T STORM OFF TO SAVE YOUR SON
I DIDN'T EVEN THINK I WAS *GOING* TO BE THE HERO, BUT THEN . . .
. . . WELL, I GUESS IT DOESN'T MATTER, DOES IT?
DON'T BE SO DOWN! I'M CERTAIN SOMEONE ***ELSE*** WILL BECOME DEATHLY ILL SOON!
HOW NICE

THREE WEEKS LATER
YOU HAVEN'T SAID MUCH ABOUT YOUR ENCOUNTER WITH THE OPENER!
WHAT'S TO SAY? HE WAS KIND OF A TWERP
THAT'S NOT NICE TO SAY WHEN HE WAS SO GENEROUS TO US
I'M NOT SAYING HE WASN'T NICE. ANYONE WELL-OFF CAN AFFORD TO BE NICE, IT DOESN'T MAKE HIM A SAINT
OH, THAT REMINDS ME!
WHAT'S THIS?
UM, INK, I GAVE THIS TO YOU
I'M ACTUALLY KINDA SURPRISED YOU DIDN'T TURN IT INTO A RELIC
I KNOW, BUT THE OPENER GAVE IT TO YOU, AND WE HAVE BLANKETS NOW, SO, IT'S YOURS AGAIN!
I'M JUST GOING TO GIVE THIS RIGHT BACK THE MOMENT YOU NEED IT!
I KNOW, HON!
HAPPY OPENERMAS!
♪
HAPPY OPENERMAS, ONE AND ALL!
RickGriffin

P.B.S.
? FREE I GUESS
This issue..... will Christmas EVER be the same?
SPOT (superdog
VS.
SANTA?!
WHAT
But why Santa? I've rescued Christmas like, so much!
orphanite candy cane
It is precisely for that reason we come to this!
DEATHTRAP
Huh? ← (spot(superdog))
You haven't saved Christmas once or twice, you've saved it TWENTY TIMES! In only five years! Making SANTA look incompetent by comparison!
Well I could, like, NOT save Christmas
WHAT?!
But saving things is what you do!
Yeah, but I wouldn't want to make Santa feel inadequate
I DONT BELIEVE YOU!
Believe me, Santa... when it comes to doing good, you are MY rolemodel!
And what happened then? Well in the North Pole they say
That the Santa's small heart grew three sizes that day!
AND SO...
Yup, a good thing was accomplished here today
AHHH
IT BURNS SO MUCH
NORTH POLE
I WORRY IF THIS'LL COME OFF AS SACRELIGIOUS
I DON'T THINK THAT'S WHAT YOU SHOULD BE WORRYING ABOUT
Next time on Spot
Punching robots!

TWO EXTRA LA-- --AAAAH-- --IS THIS THE RIGHT HOUSE?
PROBABLY! LET ME GO CHECK!
PIZZ
WHO ORDERED A WELL-MARBLED DELIVERY GUY?
COME ON! THAT WAS OBVIOUSLY A JOKE!
DO WE STILL HAVE TO PAY?

WELCOME BACK TO THE NEW YEAR'S COUNTDOWN! I'M YOUR HOST, THE CREEPY CGI RECREATION OF DICK CLARK!
OKAY HOLD ON A SECOND
WHAT'S WRONG?
SORRY, BUT YOU'RE JUST TOO CREEPY; WE'VE BEEN HEMMORAGING VIEWERS
EVERYONE PLEASE WELCOME YOUR NEW HOST, THE ROBOT CLONE OF DICK CLARK!
GREETINGS. I AM DICK CLARKTRON
HOW IS HE LESS CREEPY THAN ME?!
FOR ONE I DON'T LOOK LIKE A FLAPPING MEAT-MUPPET
AT LEAST MY BRAIN'S NOT VISIBLE IN A CLEAR GLASS DOME!
KER-FLOMP
Hold it right there you impostors!
⊰GASP⊱ THE EVIL GHOST OF DICK CLARK! I THOUGHT WE LAID YOU TO REST!
TASTE MY HOLY WATER CANNON
Curses!
Z

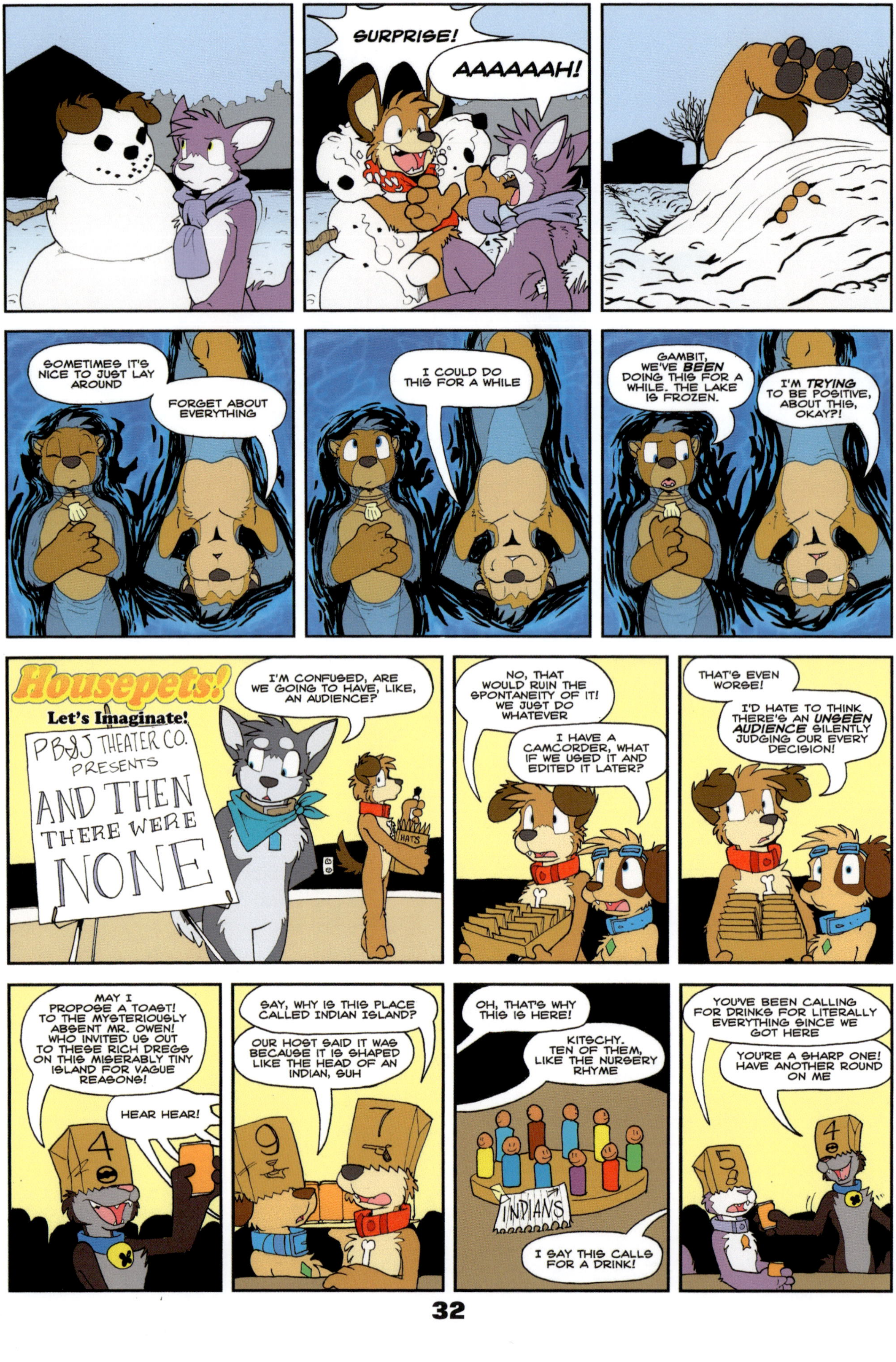
SURPRISE!
AAAAAAH!
SOMETIMES IT'S NICE TO JUST LAY AROUND
FORGET ABOUT EVERYTHING
I COULD DO THIS FOR A WHILE
GAMBIT, WE'VE BEEN DOING THIS FOR A WHILE. THE LAKE IS FROZEN.
I'M TRYING TO BE POSITIVE, ABOUT THIS, OKAY?!
Housepets!
Let's Imaginate!
PB&J THEATER CO. PRESENTS
AND THEN THERE WERE NONE
I'M CONFUSED, ARE WE GOING TO HAVE, LIKE, AN AUDIENCE?
HATS
NO, THAT WOULD RUIN THE SPONTANEITY OF IT! WE JUST DO WHATEVER
I HAVE A CAMCORDER, WHAT IF WE USED IT AND EDITED IT LATER?
THAT'S EVEN WORSE!
I'D HATE TO THINK THERE'S AN UNSEEN AUDIENCE SILENTLY JUDGING OUR EVERY DECISION!
MAY I PROPOSE A TOAST! TO THE MYSTERIOUSLY ABSENT MR. OWEN! WHO INVITED US OUT TO THESE RICH DREGS ON THIS MISERABLY TINY ISLAND FOR VAGUE REASONS!
HEAR HEAR!
4
SAY, WHY IS THIS PLACE CALLED INDIAN ISLAND?
OUR HOST SAID IT WAS BECAUSE IT IS SHAPED LIKE THE HEAD OF AN INDIAN, SUH
9
7
OH, THAT'S WHY THIS IS HERE!
KITSCHY. TEN OF THEM, LIKE THE NURSERY RHYME
INDIANS
I SAY THIS CALLS FOR A DRINK!
YOU'VE BEEN CALLING FOR DRINKS FOR LITERALLY EVERYTHING SINCE WE GOT HERE
YOU'RE A SHARP ONE! HAVE ANOTHER ROUND ON ME
5
4

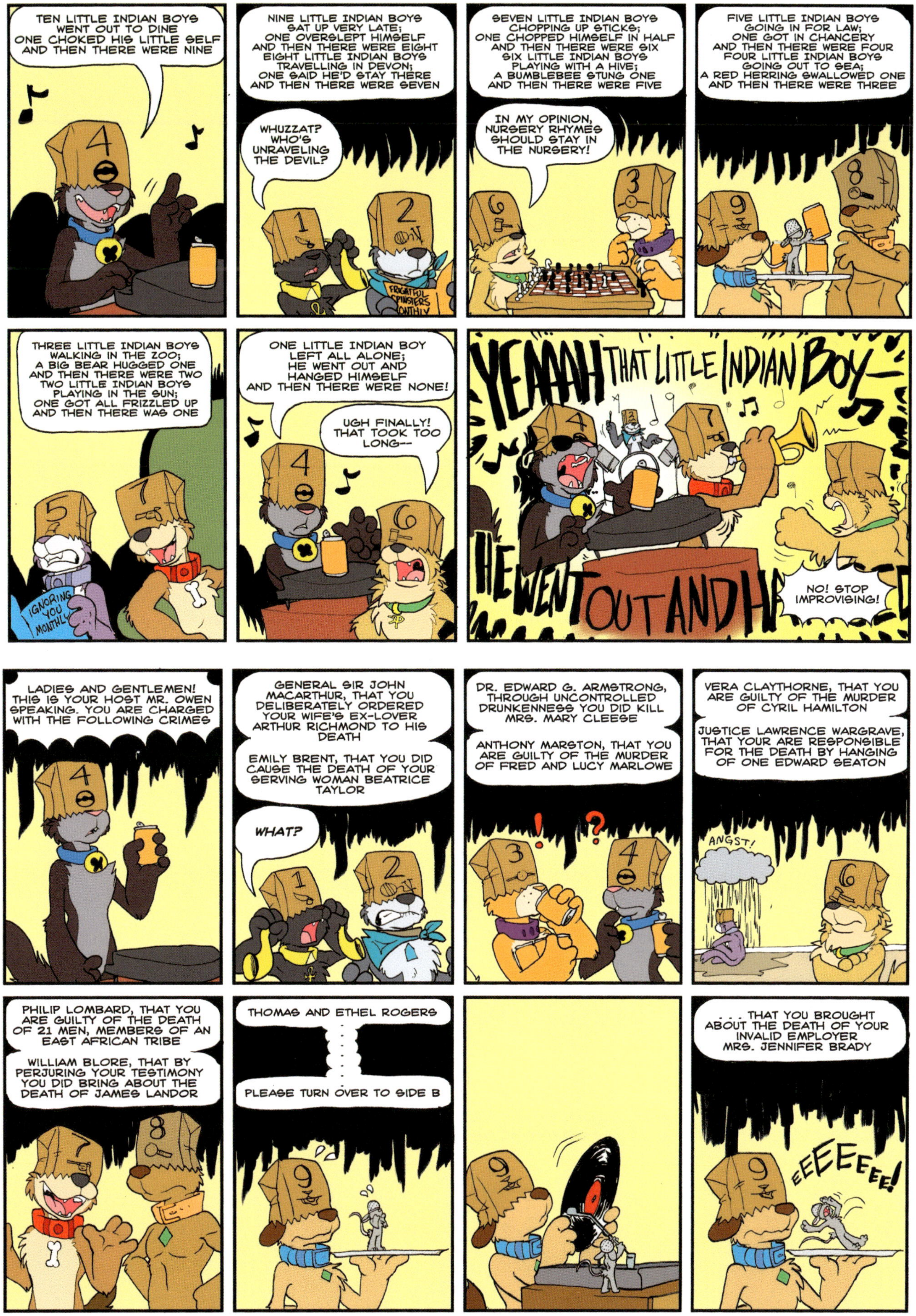
TEN LITTLE INDIAN BOYS WENT OUT TO DINE ONE CHOKED HIS LITTLE SELF AND THEN THERE WERE NINE
NINE LITTLE INDIAN BOYS SAT UP VERY LATE; ONE OVERSLEPT HIMSELF AND THEN THERE WERE EIGHT EIGHT LITTLE INDIAN BOYS TRAVELLING IN DEVON; ONE SAID HE'D STAY THERE AND THEN THERE WERE SEVEN
WHUZZAT? WHO'S UNRAVELING THE DEVIL?
FRIGHTFUL SPINSTERS MONTHLY
SEVEN LITTLE INDIAN BOYS CHOPPING UP STICKS; ONE CHOPPED HIMSELF IN HALF AND THEN THERE WERE SIX SIX LITTLE INDIAN BOYS PLAYING WITH A HIVE; A BUMBLEBEE STUNG ONE AND THEN THERE WERE FIVE
IN MY OPINION, NURSERY RHYMES SHOULD STAY IN THE NURSERY!
FIVE LITTLE INDIAN BOYS GOING IN FOR LAW; ONE GOT IN CHANCERY AND THEN THERE WERE FOUR FOUR LITTLE INDIAN BOYS GOING OUT TO SEA; A RED HERRING SWALLOWED ONE AND THEN THERE WERE THREE
THREE LITTLE INDIAN BOYS WALKING IN THE ZOO; A BIG BEAR HUGGED ONE AND THEN THERE WERE TWO TWO LITTLE INDIAN BOYS PLAYING IN THE SUN; ONE GOT ALL FRIZZLED UP AND THEN THERE WAS ONE
IGNORING YOU MONTHLY
ONE LITTLE INDIAN BOY LEFT ALL ALONE; HE WENT OUT AND HANGED HIMSELF AND THEN THERE WERE NONE!
UGH FINALLY! THAT TOOK TOO LONG--
YEAAAH THAT LITTLE INDIAN BOY—
HE WENT OUT AND H
NO! STOP IMPROVISING!
LADIES AND GENTLEMEN! THIS IS YOUR HOST MR. OWEN SPEAKING. YOU ARE CHARGED WITH THE FOLLOWING CRIMES
GENERAL SIR JOHN MACARTHUR, THAT YOU DELIBERATELY ORDERED YOUR WIFE'S EX-LOVER ARTHUR RICHMOND TO HIS DEATH
EMILY BRENT, THAT YOU DID CAUSE THE DEATH OF YOUR SERVING WOMAN BEATRICE TAYLOR
WHAT?
DR. EDWARD G. ARMSTRONG, THROUGH UNCONTROLLED DRUNKENNESS YOU DID KILL MRS. MARY CLEESE
ANTHONY MARSTON, THAT YOU ARE GUILTY OF THE MURDER OF FRED AND LUCY MARLOWE
!
?
VERA CLAYTHORNE, THAT YOU ARE GUILTY OF THE MURDER OF CYRIL HAMILTON
JUSTICE LAWRENCE WARGRAVE, THAT YOUR ARE RESPONSIBLE FOR THE DEATH BY HANGING OF ONE EDWARD SEATON
ANGST!
PHILIP LOMBARD, THAT YOU ARE GUILTY OF THE DEATH OF 21 MEN, MEMBERS OF AN EAST AFRICAN TRIBE
WILLIAM BLORE, THAT BY PERJURING YOUR TESTIMONY YOU DID BRING ABOUT THE DEATH OF JAMES LANDOR
THOMAS AND ETHEL ROGERS
PLEASE TURN OVER TO SIDE B
. . . THAT YOU BROUGHT ABOUT THE DEATH OF YOUR INVALID EMPLOYER MRS. JENNIFER BRADY
EEEEEEE!

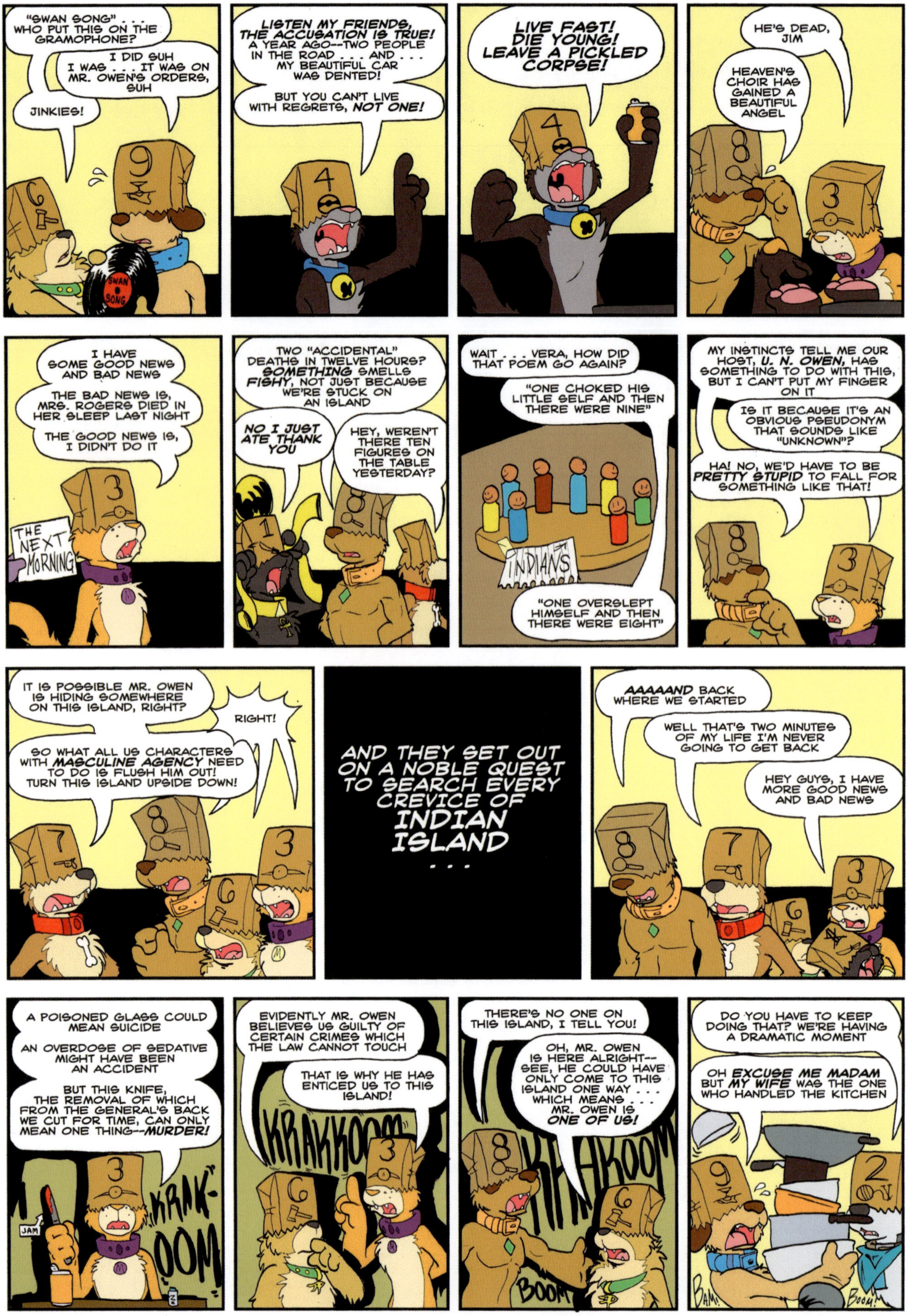
"SWAN SONG" . . . WHO PUT THIS ON THE GRAMOPHONE?
I DID SUH I WAS . . . IT WAS ON MR. OWEN'S ORDERS, SUH
JINKIES!
SWAN SONG
LISTEN MY FRIENDS, THE ACCUSATION IS TRUE! A YEAR AGO--TWO PEOPLE IN THE ROAD . . . AND . . . MY BEAUTIFUL CAR WAS DENTED!
BUT YOU CAN'T LIVE WITH REGRETS, NOT ONE!
LIVE FAST! DIE YOUNG! LEAVE A PICKLED CORPSE!
HE'S DEAD, JIM
HEAVEN'S CHOIR HAS GAINED A BEAUTIFUL ANGEL
I HAVE SOME GOOD NEWS AND BAD NEWS
THE BAD NEWS IS, MRS. ROGERS DIED IN HER SLEEP LAST NIGHT
THE GOOD NEWS IS, I DIDN'T DO IT
THE NEXT MORNING
TWO "ACCIDENTAL" DEATHS IN TWELVE HOURS? SOMETHING SMELLS FISHY, NOT JUST BECAUSE WE'RE STUCK ON AN ISLAND
NO I JUST ATE THANK YOU
HEY, WEREN'T THERE TEN FIGURES ON THE TABLE YESTERDAY?
WAIT . . . VERA, HOW DID THAT POEM GO AGAIN?
"ONE CHOKED HIS LITTLE SELF AND THEN THERE WERE NINE"
INDIANS
"ONE OVERSLEPT HIMSELF AND THEN THERE WERE EIGHT"
MY INSTINCTS TELL ME OUR HOST, U. N. OWEN, HAS SOMETHING TO DO WITH THIS, BUT I CAN'T PUT MY FINGER ON IT
IS IT BECAUSE IT'S AN OBVIOUS PSEUDONYM THAT SOUNDS LIKE "UNKNOWN"?
HA! NO, WE'D HAVE TO BE PRETTY STUPID TO FALL FOR SOMETHING LIKE THAT!
IT IS POSSIBLE MR. OWEN IS HIDING SOMEWHERE ON THIS ISLAND, RIGHT?
RIGHT!
SO WHAT ALL US CHARACTERS WITH MASCULINE AGENCY NEED TO DO IS FLUSH HIM OUT! TURN THIS ISLAND UPSIDE DOWN!
AND THEY SET OUT ON A NOBLE QUEST TO SEARCH EVERY CREVICE OF INDIAN ISLAND . . .
AAAAAND BACK WHERE WE STARTED
WELL THAT'S TWO MINUTES OF MY LIFE I'M NEVER GOING TO GET BACK
HEY GUYS, I HAVE MORE GOOD NEWS AND BAD NEWS
A POISONED GLASS COULD MEAN SUICIDE
AN OVERDOSE OF SEDATIVE MIGHT HAVE BEEN AN ACCIDENT
BUT THIS KNIFE, THE REMOVAL OF WHICH FROM THE GENERAL'S BACK WE CUT FOR TIME, CAN ONLY MEAN ONE THING--MURDER!
JAM
KRAK-OOM
EVIDENTLY MR. OWEN BELIEVES US GUILTY OF CERTAIN CRIMES WHICH THE LAW CANNOT TOUCH
THAT IS WHY HE HAS ENTICED US TO THIS ISLAND!
KRAKKOOM
THERE'S NO ONE ON THIS ISLAND, I TELL YOU!
OH, MR. OWEN IS HERE ALRIGHT--SEE, HE COULD HAVE ONLY COME TO THIS ISLAND ONE WAY . . . WHICH MEANS . . . MR. OWEN IS ONE OF US!
KRAKOOM
BOOM
DO YOU HAVE TO KEEP DOING THAT? WE'RE HAVING A DRAMATIC MOMENT
OH EXCUSE ME MADAM BUT MY WIFE WAS THE ONE WHO HANDLED THE KITCHEN
BAM!
BOOM!

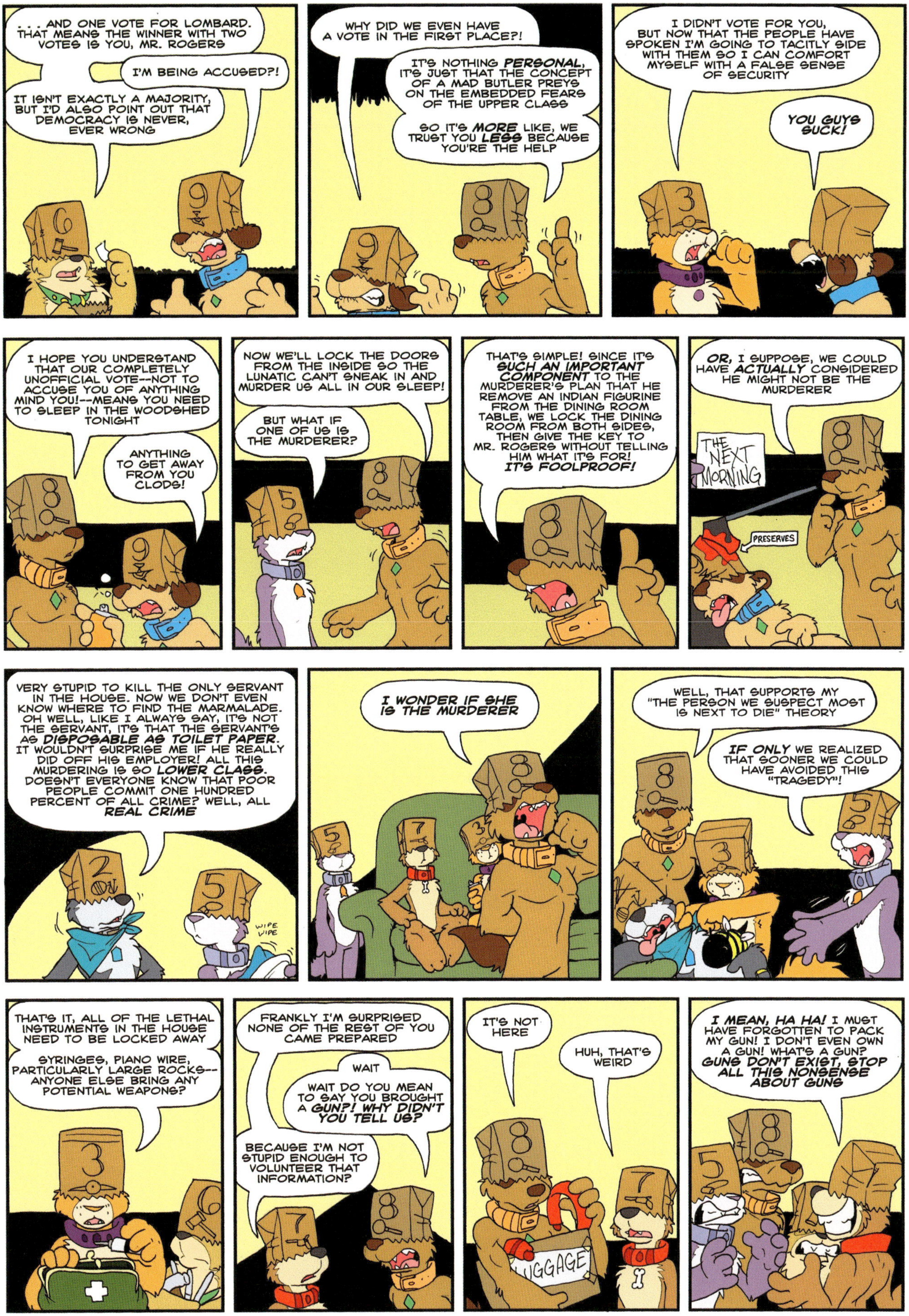
. . . AND ONE VOTE FOR LOMBARD. THAT MEANS THE WINNER WITH TWO VOTES IS YOU, MR. ROGERS
I'M BEING ACCUSED?!
IT ISN'T EXACTLY A MAJORITY, BUT I'D ALSO POINT OUT THAT DEMOCRACY IS NEVER, EVER WRONG
WHY DID WE EVEN HAVE A VOTE IN THE FIRST PLACE?!
IT'S NOTHING PERSONAL, IT'S JUST THAT THE CONCEPT OF A MAD BUTLER PREYS ON THE EMBEDDED FEARS OF THE UPPER CLASS
SO IT'S MORE LIKE, WE TRUST YOU LESS BECAUSE YOU'RE THE HELP
I DIDN'T VOTE FOR YOU, BUT NOW THAT THE PEOPLE HAVE SPOKEN I'M GOING TO TACITLY SIDE WITH THEM SO I CAN COMFORT MYSELF WITH A FALSE SENSE OF SECURITY
YOU GUYS SUCK!
I HOPE YOU UNDERSTAND THAT OUR COMPLETELY UNOFFICIAL VOTE--NOT TO ACCUSE YOU OF ANYTHING MIND YOU!--MEANS YOU NEED TO SLEEP IN THE WOODSHED TONIGHT
ANYTHING TO GET AWAY FROM YOU CLODS!
NOW WE'LL LOCK THE DOORS FROM THE INSIDE SO THE LUNATIC CAN'T SNEAK IN AND MURDER US ALL IN OUR SLEEP!
BUT WHAT IF ONE OF US IS THE MURDERER?
THAT'S SIMPLE! SINCE IT'S SUCH AN IMPORTANT COMPONENT TO THE MURDERER'S PLAN THAT HE REMOVE AN INDIAN FIGURINE FROM THE DINING ROOM TABLE, WE LOCK THE DINING ROOM FROM BOTH SIDES, THEN GIVE THE KEY TO MR. ROGERS WITHOUT TELLING HIM WHAT IT'S FOR! IT'S FOOLPROOF!
OR, I SUPPOSE, WE COULD HAVE ACTUALLY CONSIDERED HE MIGHT NOT BE THE MURDERER
THE NEXT MORNING
PRESERVES
VERY STUPID TO KILL THE ONLY SERVANT IN THE HOUSE. NOW WE DON'T EVEN KNOW WHERE TO FIND THE MARMALADE. OH WELL, LIKE I ALWAYS SAY, IT'S NOT THE SERVANT, IT'S THAT THE SERVANT'S AS DISPOSABLE AS TOILET PAPER. IT WOULDN'T SURPRISE ME IF HE REALLY DID OFF HIS EMPLOYER! ALL THIS MURDERING IS SO LOWER CLASS. DOESN'T EVERYONE KNOW THAT POOR PEOPLE COMMIT ONE HUNDRED PERCENT OF ALL CRIME? WELL, ALL REAL CRIME
WIPE WIPE
I WONDER IF SHE IS THE MURDERER
WELL, THAT SUPPORTS MY "THE PERSON WE SUSPECT MOST IS NEXT TO DIE" THEORY
IF ONLY WE REALIZED THAT SOONER WE COULD HAVE AVOIDED THIS "TRAGEDY"!
THAT'S IT, ALL OF THE LETHAL INSTRUMENTS IN THE HOUSE NEED TO BE LOCKED AWAY
SYRINGES, PIANO WIRE, PARTICULARLY LARGE ROCKS--ANYONE ELSE BRING ANY POTENTIAL WEAPONS?
FRANKLY I'M SURPRISED NONE OF THE REST OF YOU CAME PREPARED
WAIT
WAIT DO YOU MEAN TO SAY YOU BROUGHT A GUN?! WHY DIDN'T YOU TELL US?
BECAUSE I'M NOT STUPID ENOUGH TO VOLUNTEER THAT INFORMATION?
IT'S NOT HERE
HUH, THAT'S WEIRD
UGGAGE
I MEAN, HA HA! I MUST HAVE FORGOTTEN TO PACK MY GUN! I DON'T EVEN OWN A GUN! WHAT'S A GUN? GUNS DON'T EXIST, STOP ALL THIS NONSENSE ABOUT GUNS

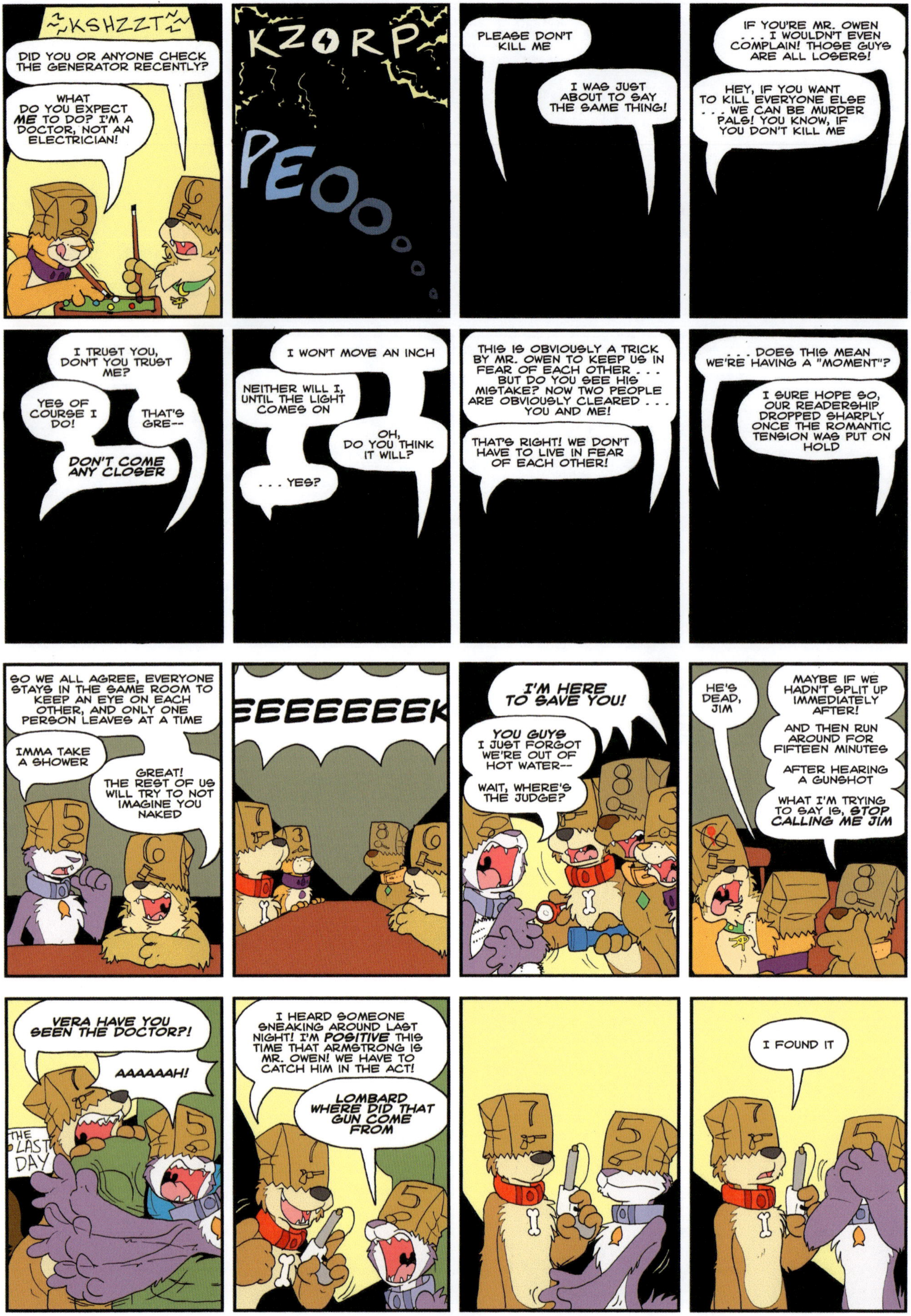
~KSHZZT~
DID YOU OR ANYONE CHECK THE GENERATOR RECENTLY?
WHAT DO YOU EXPECT ME TO DO? I'M A DOCTOR, NOT AN ELECTRICIAN!
KZORP
PEOOOOOO
PLEASE DON'T KILL ME
I WAS JUST ABOUT TO SAY THE SAME THING!
IF YOU'RE MR. OWEN . . . I WOULDN'T EVEN COMPLAIN! THOSE GUYS ARE ALL LOSERS!
HEY, IF YOU WANT TO KILL EVERYONE ELSE . . . WE CAN BE MURDER PALS! YOU KNOW, IF YOU DON'T KILL ME
I TRUST YOU, DON'T YOU TRUST ME?
YES OF COURSE I DO!
THAT'S GRE--
DON'T COME ANY CLOSER
I WON'T MOVE AN INCH
NEITHER WILL I, UNTIL THE LIGHT COMES ON
OH, DO YOU THINK IT WILL?
. . . YES?
THIS IS OBVIOUSLY A TRICK BY MR. OWEN TO KEEP US IN FEAR OF EACH OTHER . . . BUT DO YOU SEE HIS MISTAKE? NOW TWO PEOPLE ARE OBVIOUSLY CLEARED . . . YOU AND ME!
THAT'S RIGHT! WE DON'T HAVE TO LIVE IN FEAR OF EACH OTHER!
. . . DOES THIS MEAN WE'RE HAVING A "MOMENT"?
I SURE HOPE SO, OUR READERSHIP DROPPED SHARPLY ONCE THE ROMANTIC TENSION WAS PUT ON HOLD
SO WE ALL AGREE, EVERYONE STAYS IN THE SAME ROOM TO KEEP AN EYE ON EACH OTHER, AND ONLY ONE PERSON LEAVES AT A TIME
IMMA TAKE A SHOWER
GREAT! THE REST OF US WILL TRY TO NOT IMAGINE YOU NAKED
EEEEEEEEK
I'M HERE TO SAVE YOU!
YOU GUYS I JUST FORGOT WE'RE OUT OF HOT WATER--
WAIT, WHERE'S THE JUDGE?
HE'S DEAD, JIM
MAYBE IF WE HADN'T SPLIT UP IMMEDIATELY AFTER!
AND THEN RUN AROUND FOR FIFTEEN MINUTES
AFTER HEARING A GUNSHOT
WHAT I'M TRYING TO SAY IS, STOP CALLING ME JIM
VERA HAVE YOU SEEN THE DOCTOR?!
AAAAAAAH!
THE LAST DAY
I HEARD SOMEONE SNEAKING AROUND LAST NIGHT! I'M POSITIVE THIS TIME THAT ARMSTRONG IS MR. OWEN! WE HAVE TO CATCH HIM IN THE ACT!
LOMBARD WHERE DID THAT GUN COME FROM
I FOUND IT

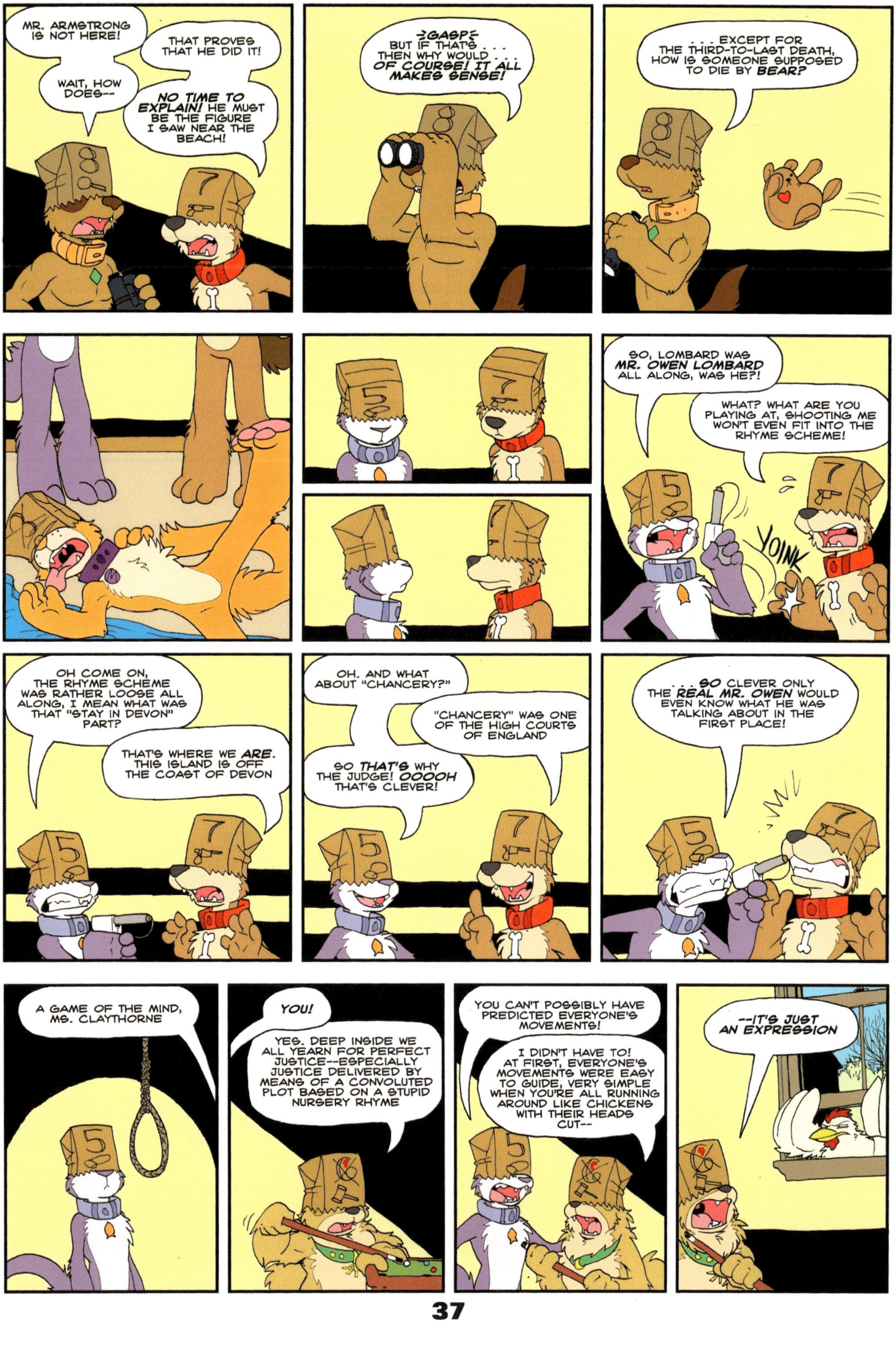
MR. ARMSTRONG IS NOT HERE!
THAT PROVES THAT HE DID IT!
WAIT, HOW DOES--
NO TIME TO EXPLAIN! HE MUST BE THE FIGURE I SAW NEAR THE BEACH!
≥GASP≤ BUT IF THAT'S . . . THEN WHY WOULD . . . OF COURSE! IT ALL MAKES SENSE!
. . . EXCEPT FOR THE THIRD-TO-LAST DEATH, HOW IS SOMEONE SUPPOSED TO DIE BY BEAR?
SO, LOMBARD WAS MR. OWEN LOMBARD ALL ALONG, WAS HE?!
WHAT? WHAT ARE YOU PLAYING AT, SHOOTING ME WON'T EVEN FIT INTO THE RHYME SCHEME!
YOINK
OH COME ON, THE RHYME SCHEME WAS RATHER LOOSE ALL ALONG, I MEAN WHAT WAS THAT "STAY IN DEVON" PART?
THAT'S WHERE WE ARE. THIS ISLAND IS OFF THE COAST OF DEVON
OH. AND WHAT ABOUT "CHANCERY?"
"CHANCERY" WAS ONE OF THE HIGH COURTS OF ENGLAND
SO THAT'S WHY THE JUDGE! OOOOH THAT'S CLEVER!
. . . SO CLEVER ONLY THE REAL MR. OWEN WOULD EVEN KNOW WHAT HE WAS TALKING ABOUT IN THE FIRST PLACE!
A GAME OF THE MIND, MS. CLAYTHORNE
YOU!
YES. DEEP INSIDE WE ALL YEARN FOR PERFECT JUSTICE--ESPECIALLY JUSTICE DELIVERED BY MEANS OF A CONVOLUTED PLOT BASED ON A STUPID NURSERY RHYME
YOU CAN'T POSSIBLY HAVE PREDICTED EVERYONE'S MOVEMENTS!
I DIDN'T HAVE TO! AT FIRST, EVERYONE'S MOVEMENTS WERE EASY TO GUIDE, VERY SIMPLE WHEN YOU'RE ALL RUNNING AROUND LIKE CHICKENS WITH THEIR HEADS CUT--
--IT'S JUST AN EXPRESSION

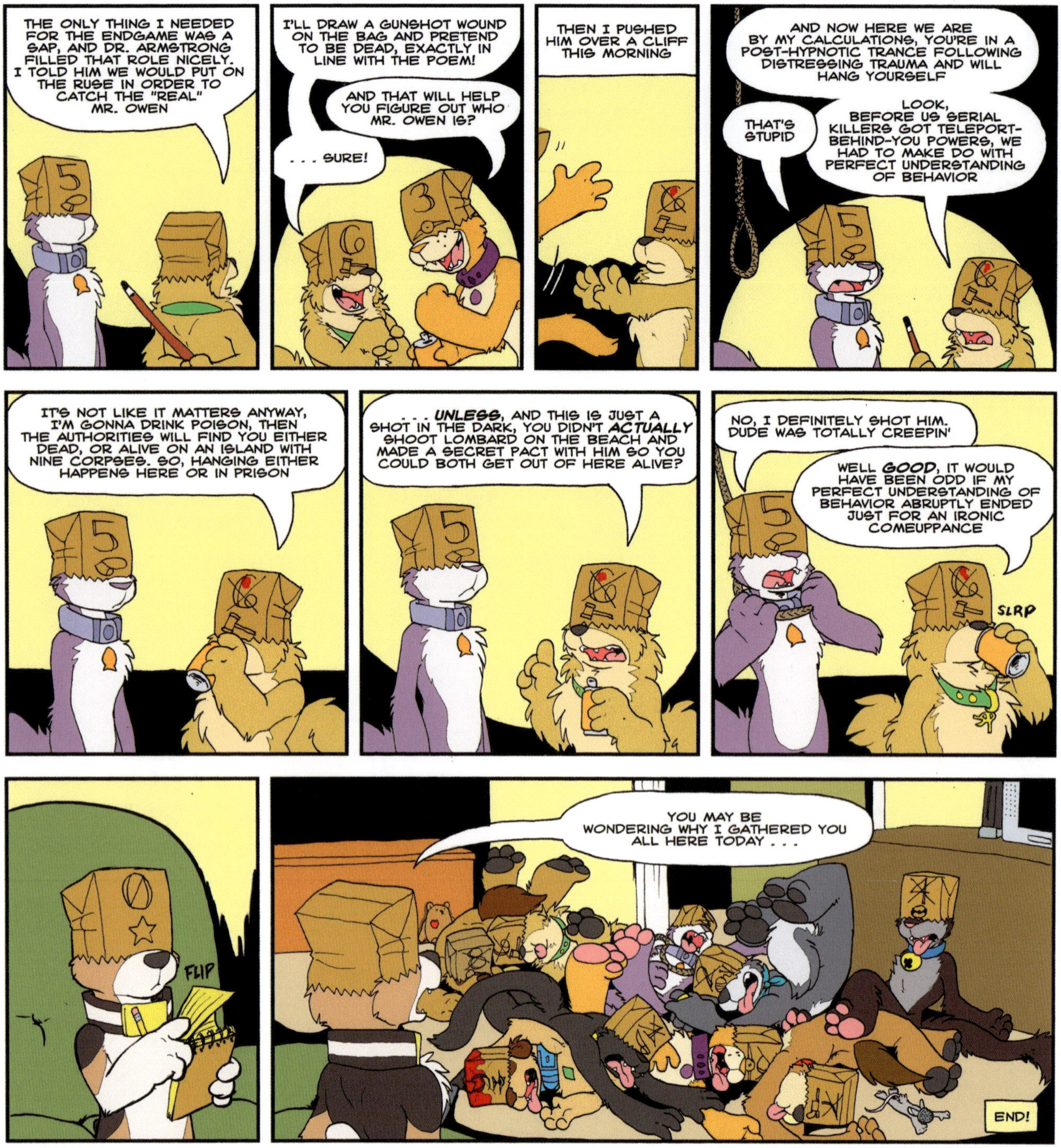
THE ONLY THING I NEEDED FOR THE ENDGAME WAS A SAP, AND DR. ARMSTRONG FILLED THAT ROLE NICELY. I TOLD HIM WE WOULD PUT ON THE RUSE IN ORDER TO CATCH THE "REAL" MR. OWEN
I'LL DRAW A GUNSHOT WOUND ON THE BAG AND PRETEND TO BE DEAD, EXACTLY IN LINE WITH THE POEM!
AND THAT WILL HELP YOU FIGURE OUT WHO MR. OWEN IS?
. . . SURE!
THEN I PUSHED HIM OVER A CLIFF THIS MORNING
AND NOW HERE WE ARE BY MY CALCULATIONS, YOU'RE IN A POST-HYPNOTIC TRANCE FOLLOWING DISTRESSING TRAUMA AND WILL HANG YOURSELF
THAT'S STUPID
LOOK, BEFORE US SERIAL KILLERS GOT TELEPORT-BEHIND-YOU POWERS, WE HAD TO MAKE DO WITH PERFECT UNDERSTANDING OF BEHAVIOR
IT'S NOT LIKE IT MATTERS ANYWAY, I'M GONNA DRINK POISON, THEN THE AUTHORITIES WILL FIND YOU EITHER DEAD, OR ALIVE ON AN ISLAND WITH NINE CORPSES. SO, HANGING EITHER HAPPENS HERE OR IN PRISON
. . . UNLESS, AND THIS IS JUST A SHOT IN THE DARK, YOU DIDN'T ACTUALLY SHOOT LOMBARD ON THE BEACH AND MADE A SECRET PACT WITH HIM SO YOU COULD BOTH GET OUT OF HERE ALIVE?
NO, I DEFINITELY SHOT HIM. DUDE WAS TOTALLY CREEPIN'
WELL GOOD, IT WOULD HAVE BEEN ODD IF MY PERFECT UNDERSTANDING OF BEHAVIOR ABRUPTLY ENDED JUST FOR AN IRONIC COMEUPPANCE
SLRP
FLIP
YOU MAY BE WONDERING WHY I GATHERED YOU ALL HERE TODAY . . .
END!

KEVIN I WANT TO GET THAT CAR SHAPED LIKE A KETCHUP BOTTLE AND DRIVE AROUND BEHIND THE WEINERMOBILE!
SASHA, DO YOU REALIZE WHAT YOU'RE SAYING?
BECAUSE IT SOUNDS AWESOME!
EEEE!
OH WAIT, NO, NEITHER OF US CAN DRIVE
WE HAVE LICENSES, SILLY!
IT'S A DOG LICENSE, SASHA!
THAT MEANS WE CAN ONLY DRIVE CARS THAT ARE SHAPED LIKE DOGS
I THINK WE CAN MAKE THAT WORK

© 2014 Rick Griffin
http://www.housepetscomic.com
LOVE SUCKS
LET'S TRY IT ANYWAY

© 2014 Rick Griffin
Some small part of me wants to be your Valentine, and I can't get it to shut up
http://www.housepetscomic.com

© 2014 Rick Griffin
http://www.housepetscomic.com
What?

© 2014 Rick Griffin
WITH ALL SINCERE GRACE AND HUMILITY, I WILL ALLOW YOU THE HONOR OF BEING MY VALENTINE
http://www.housepetscomic.com

MAN DID YOU SEE THIS
YEAH I KNOW! JAPAN, RIGHT? THEY'RE SO WEIRD!
ISHA O YONDE!
E, YOU REALIZE THAT'S A COMEDY SHOW, NE? THERE'S JUST AS MANY DUMB THINGS ON AMERICAN TELEVISION, BUT WHEN IT COMES TO A FOREIGN CULTURE, SUDDENLY IT CAN'T POSSIBLY BE FUNNY ON PURPOSE
HEY, I'M NOT SAYING IT'S NOT FUNNY, IT'S JUST FREAKY WEIRD!
WHAT'D YOU BRING FOR LUNCH?
A DISAPPOINTMENT! YOU WOULDN'T BELIEVE HOW HARD IT IS TO FIND SQUID EYEBALLS AND BEE LARVAE AROUND HERE!
YOU SEE WHAT I MEAN?!
MEN

I BROUGHT YOU A SANDWICH!
OH, COOL!
SAY, WHAT'S THE WEIRDEST THING YOU'VE EVER EATEN?
WELL I ATE ONE OF THOSE MOCHACCINO BURRITOS ONCE, BUT I'M GONNA HAVE TO SAY DOLPHIN
THOUGH I'D RATHER NOT ELABORATE
. . . WHY DO YOU ASK?
NO REASON

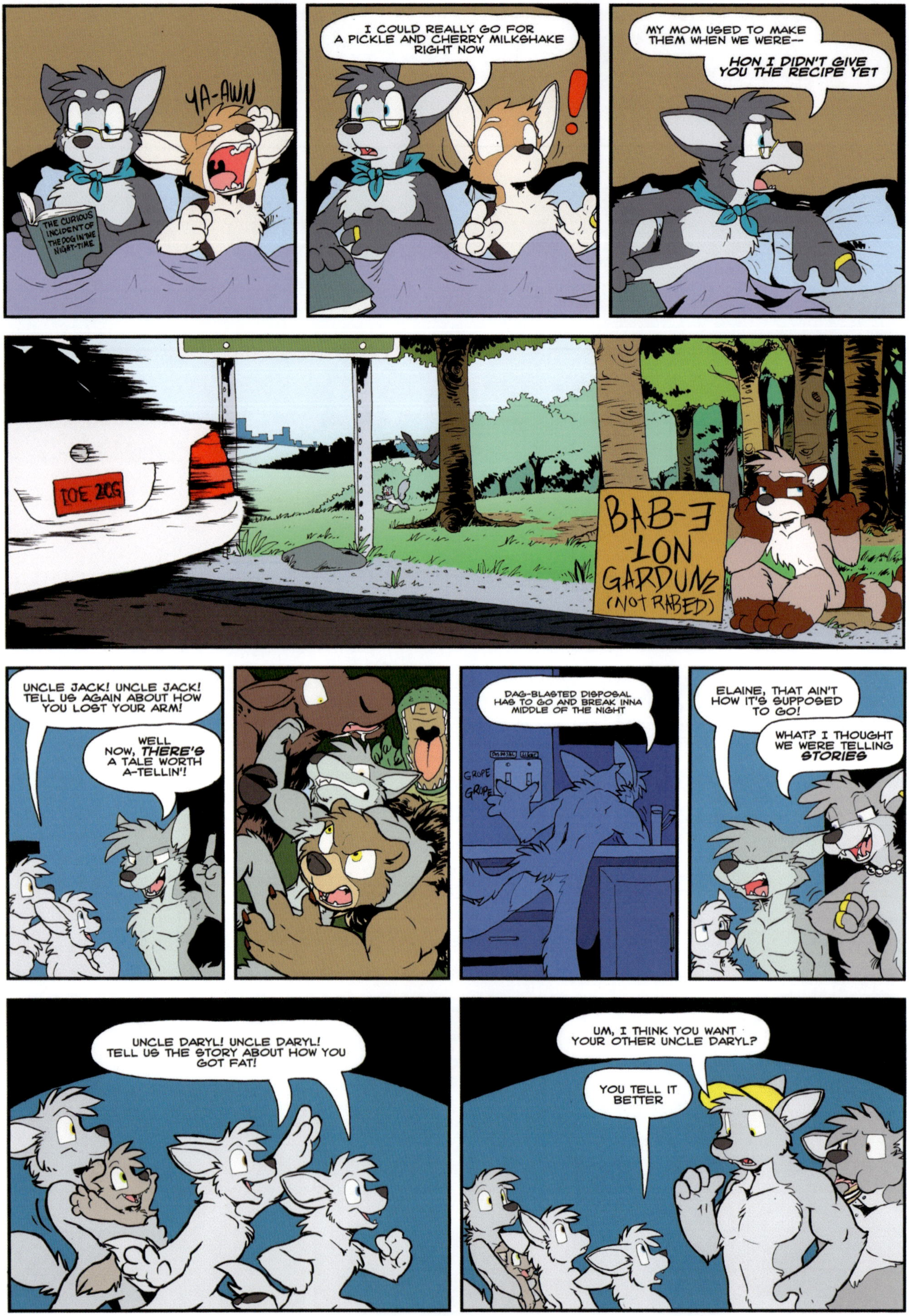
THE CURIOUS INCIDENT OF THE DOG IN THE NIGHT-TIME
YA-AWN
I COULD REALLY GO FOR A PICKLE AND CHERRY MILKSHAKE RIGHT NOW
!
MY MOM USED TO MAKE THEM WHEN WE WERE--
HON I DIDN'T GIVE YOU THE RECIPE YET
IOE 2CG
BAB-E -LON GARDUNZ (NOT RABED)
UNCLE JACK! UNCLE JACK! TELL US AGAIN ABOUT HOW YOU LOST YOUR ARM!
WELL NOW, THERE'S A TALE WORTH A-TELLIN'!
DAG-BLASTED DISPOSAL HAS TO GO AND BREAK INNA MIDDLE OF THE NIGHT
GROPE
GROPE
ELAINE, THAT AIN'T HOW IT'S SUPPOSED TO GO!
WHAT? I THOUGHT WE WERE TELLING STORIES
UNCLE DARYL! UNCLE DARYL! TELL US THE STORY ABOUT HOW YOU GOT FAT!
UM, I THINK YOU WANT YOUR OTHER UNCLE DARYL?
YOU TELL IT BETTER

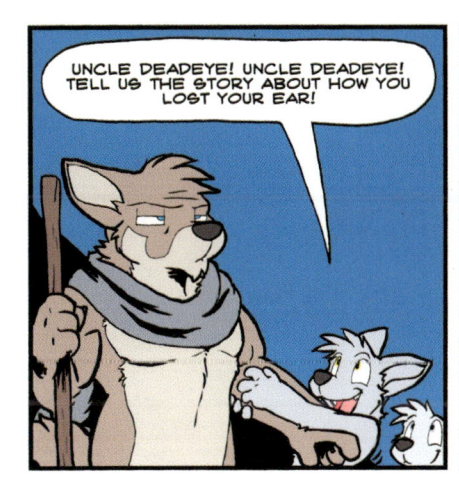

Panel 1: UNCLE DEADEYE! UNCLE DEADEYE! TELL US THE STORY ABOUT HOW YOU LOST YOUR EAR!

Panel 3: THIS IS MY FAVORITE PART

Center: HEY KIDS! DO YOU WANT TO HEAR *MY* STORIE--

NO THANKS

Panel 4: KARI! WHAT IN THE WORLD ARE THOSE?! / RADIO TRACKING COLLARS!

Panel 5: ISN'T *ONE* OF THOSE ENOUGH TO KEEP TABS ON YOU? / OH KEENE, YOU'RE SO FUNNY

Panel 6: BESIDES, SHOULDN'T YOU BE *LESS* WORRIED ABOUT ME, AND *MORE* WORRIED ABOUT WHERE TWO DOZEN UNCONTROLLED MOUNTAIN LIONS ARE?

ZIP!

WOAH-HO! YOU'RE LISTENING TO THE MORNING EXPOSITION HOUR ON WPIT WITH YOUR HOSTS SPONGECAKE AND THE CROM!
WE HAVE OUR WACKY UNCOMFORTABLE CRANK CALLS COMING UP, BUT FIRST WE HAVE THE LIVE RESULTS FROM OUR DRAWING FOR YOUR VERY OWN TV SHOW!
AOOOOOOOOOGAH!
OUR ARTISTIC BROTHER IS STARTING HIS OWN TELEVISION NETWORK BUT UH-OH!
WAH-WAAAAAAH
IT TURNS OUT FIVE PERCENT OF AIRTIME MUST CONTAIN EDUCATIONAL CONTENT!
BOOOOOOOOOO!
THAT'S AN HOUR AND FIFTEEN MINUTES TO FILL EVERY DAY AND HE LOOKED TO YOU TO SHOW YOUR CHOPS!
HAAAAI-YA!
IT WAS AN OPEN BALLOT TO ANYONE AND EVERYONE,
DEMOCRACY
ALL THAT MATTERED IS WHICH LOCAL HERO YOU WANTED TO SEE ON THE AIR!
FANFARE NOISES
LET'S NOW GO LIVE TO THE DRAWING OUTSIDE THE NEW BROADCAST STATION!
WHO THE DOOK IS "THE OPENER OF WAYS"?
YOUR NAME-SLASH-MONIKER CAME UP IN THE FIRST THIRTY SHUFFLES, AND OUR BACKUP STRATEGY SHOWED YOU GOT 93% OF THE VOTE
BUT I DON'T WANT A TV SHOW!
TECHNICALLY, THE TERMS OF THE BALLOT IS THAT THE VOTE IS FOR EACH HOUSEHOLD, SO--
DID SOMEONE SAY TV SHOW?!
WOULD YOU LIKE TO TAKE THE RABBIT'S PLACE, THEN?
TOUGH CALL! ON THE ONE HAND, I FINALLY GET ACCOLADES FOR MY UNCHARTED BRILLIANCE. ON THE OTHER HAND, IT MEANS I HAVE TO COMMUTE--
WAIT, THIS WILL GET HIM OUT OF THE HOUSE?!
BEFORE WE GET STARTED WE HAVE SOME PAPERWORK TO GET THROUGH--THIS IS VERY IMPORTANT, SO PLEASE, DON'T HESITATE TO ASK ANY QUESTIONS
YOU DON'T HAVE TO HOLD MY HAND! I'M NOT AN IDIOT!
FIRST IS THE WAIVER IN CASE OF CRIMINAL MISCONDUCT
Housepets!
Tiger's Very Own Super Special Television Show!
ACCIDENT WAIVER
SIGN
SIGN
MEDICAL WAIVER
WAIVE CONTRACT NEGOTIATION RIGHTS AND CEDE THEM TO THE STUDIO
SIGN
WAIVE RIGHT TO FILING CIVIL OR CRIMINAL CHARGES AGAINST THE STUDIO
SIGN
RELINQUISH WAGES IN CASE OF DAMAGES TO--
HOLD IT RIGHT THERE!
. . . WHAT'S "RELINQUISH"?
THAT MEANS "WAIVE"
HA! YOU WEREN'T GOING TO SNEAK THAT ONE PAST ME!
SIGN

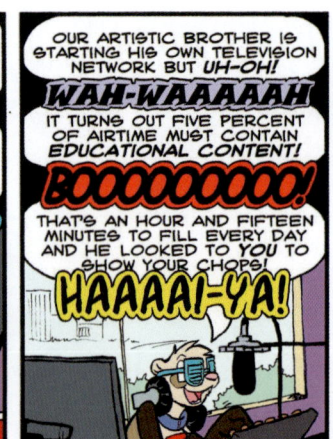

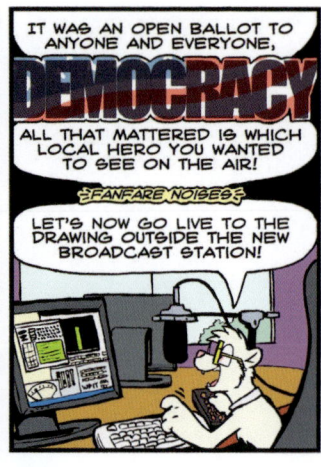

TAH-DAAH!
YOUR ONE AND ONLY MASTER OF CEREMONIES IS--
BAAM
. . . WAIT, WHERE'S THE AUDIENCE?
YAY!
A STUDIO AUDIENCE IS A LITIGATION NIGHTMARE WAITING TO HAPPEN!
BUT YOU DO HAVE A "LIVE AUDIENCE", THEY'RE WATCHING VIA SATELLITE FEED
I'M COLD!
WHO'S THE WEIRD MOOSE?
I WANT MY MOMMY!
YOU PROMISED US SNACKS!
OH, AND THE PRESHOW ENDED ABOUT HALF AN HOUR AGO, SO THEY'RE ALL WARMED UP FOR YOU! BREAK A LEG!
HEY KIDS! IT'S TIME FOR
The Funtime Learning Hour or so!
WITH YOUR HOST, ARCHIBALD THE DOG!
WAIT, WHAT?
HEY KIDDIES! ARE YOU READY TO LEARN!?
MAYBE
YEAH!
I DUNNO
GEORGE WASHINGTON!
THEN LET'S TURN TO THE WHEEL OF THINGS!
WIZZZZ!
OHHHH . . . WHEEL OF THINGS WON'T YOU TURN FOR US? THE LESSON FOR TODAY IS--
DIFFERENTIAL CALCULUS
UH . . .
OH, SORRY, WE REPURPOSED THE WHEEL FROM OUR OLD DARTBOARD. WE MEANT FOR THAT TO LAND ON "CATS"
GRAB BAG IT IS, THEN!
TODAY'S EPISODE IS BROUGHT TO YOU BY THE LETTER P!
WHAT WORD AM I THINKING OF THAT STARTS WITH THE LETTER P?
POPCORN!
PANTS!
PICKLE?
PICARD!
PUSILLANIMOUS!
GEORGE WASHINGTON!
PURPLE!
KNOCK KNOCK KNOCK KNOCK
WHO COULD THAT BE?!
HEY KIDS! IT'S CHAUNCEY, THE BACKFLIPPING ROBOT PENGUIN!
YAAAAAY!
WAK WAK WAK
FLIP
YAY!
WILD APPLAUSE
CHEER!
CLAP CLAP CLAP CLAP CLAP CLAP CLAP
WAK WAK WAK
CHAUNCEY, WHAT WORD DO YOU KNOW THAT STARTS WITH THE LETTER P?
PANDEMONIUM

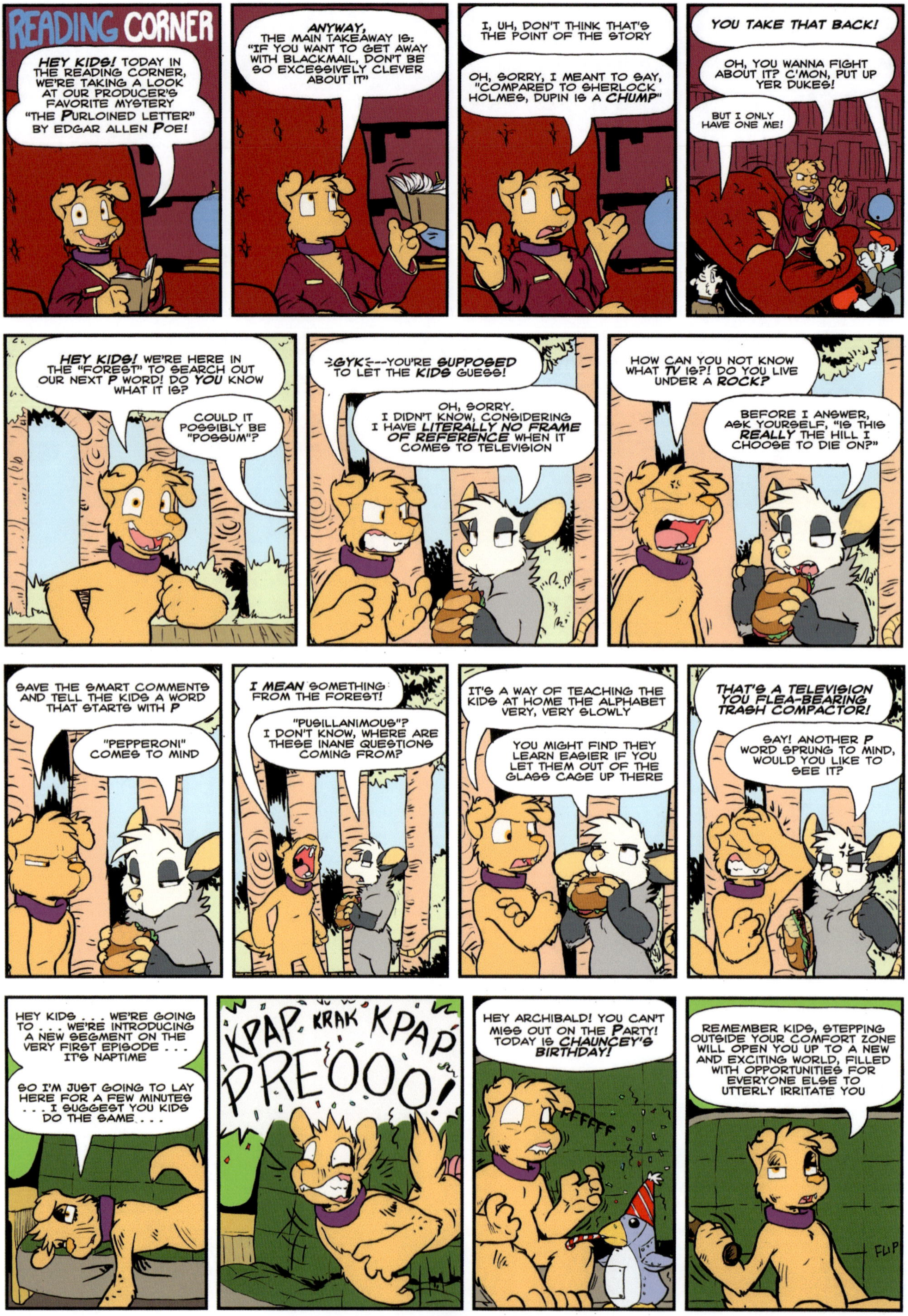
READING CORNER
HEY KIDS! TODAY IN THE READING CORNER, WE'RE TAKING A LOOK AT OUR PRODUCER'S FAVORITE MYSTERY "THE PURLOINED LETTER" BY EDGAR ALLEN POE!
ANYWAY, THE MAIN TAKEAWAY IS: "IF YOU WANT TO GET AWAY WITH BLACKMAIL, DON'T BE SO EXCESSIVELY CLEVER ABOUT IT"
I, UH, DON'T THINK THAT'S THE POINT OF THE STORY
OH, SORRY, I MEANT TO SAY, "COMPARED TO SHERLOCK HOLMES, DUPIN IS A CHUMP"
YOU TAKE THAT BACK!
OH, YOU WANNA FIGHT ABOUT IT? C'MON, PUT UP YER DUKES!
BUT I ONLY HAVE ONE ME!
HEY KIDS! WE'RE HERE IN THE "FOREST" TO SEARCH OUT OUR NEXT P WORD! DO YOU KNOW WHAT IT IS?
COULD IT POSSIBLY BE "POSSUM"?
GYK---YOU'RE SUPPOSED TO LET THE KIDS GUESS!
OH, SORRY. I DIDN'T KNOW, CONSIDERING I HAVE LITERALLY NO FRAME OF REFERENCE WHEN IT COMES TO TELEVISION
HOW CAN YOU NOT KNOW WHAT TV IS?! DO YOU LIVE UNDER A ROCK?
BEFORE I ANSWER, ASK YOURSELF, "IS THIS REALLY THE HILL I CHOOSE TO DIE ON?"
SAVE THE SMART COMMENTS AND TELL THE KIDS A WORD THAT STARTS WITH P
"PEPPERONI" COMES TO MIND
I MEAN SOMETHING FROM THE FOREST!
"PUSILLANIMOUS"? I DON'T KNOW, WHERE ARE THESE INANE QUESTIONS COMING FROM?
IT'S A WAY OF TEACHING THE KIDS AT HOME THE ALPHABET VERY, VERY SLOWLY
YOU MIGHT FIND THEY LEARN EASIER IF YOU LET THEM OUT OF THE GLASS CAGE UP THERE
THAT'S A TELEVISION YOU FLEA-BEARING TRASH COMPACTOR!
SAY! ANOTHER P WORD SPRUNG TO MIND, WOULD YOU LIKE TO SEE IT?
HEY KIDS . . . WE'RE GOING TO . . . WE'RE INTRODUCING A NEW SEGMENT ON THE VERY FIRST EPISODE . . . IT'S NAPTIME
SO I'M JUST GOING TO LAY HERE FOR A FEW MINUTES . . . I SUGGEST YOU KIDS DO THE SAME . . .
KPAP KRAK KPAP
PREOOO!
HEY ARCHIBALD! YOU CAN'T MISS OUT ON THE PARTY! TODAY IS CHAUNCEY'S BIRTHDAY!
FFFFFF
REMEMBER KIDS, STEPPING OUTSIDE YOUR COMFORT ZONE WILL OPEN YOU UP TO A NEW AND EXCITING WORLD, FILLED WITH OPPORTUNITIES FOR EVERYONE ELSE TO UTTERLY IRRITATE YOU
FLIP

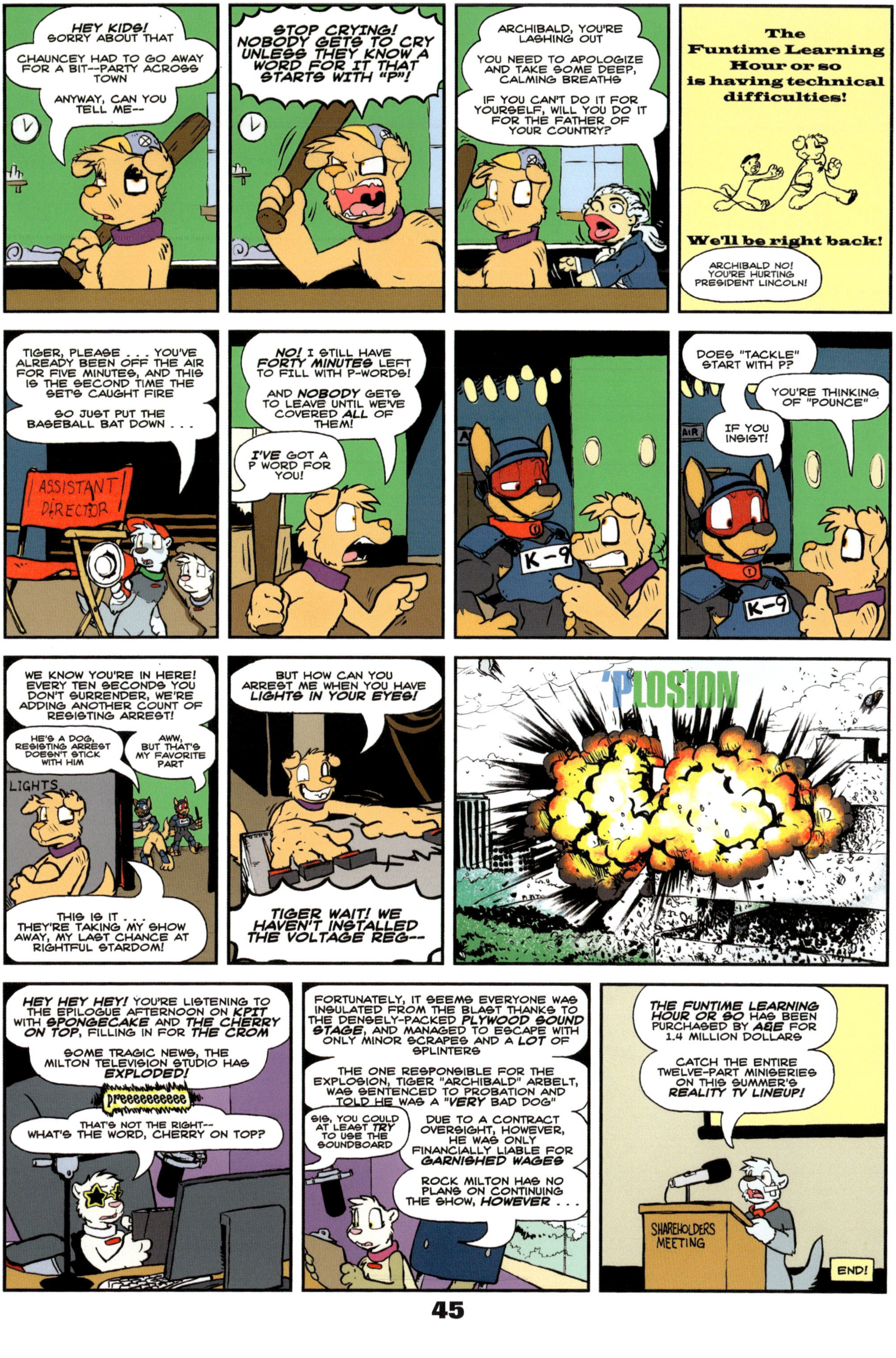
HEY KIDS! SORRY ABOUT THAT
CHAUNCEY HAD TO GO AWAY FOR A BIT--PARTY ACROSS TOWN
ANYWAY, CAN YOU TELL ME--
STOP CRYING! NOBODY GETS TO CRY UNLESS THEY KNOW A WORD FOR IT THAT STARTS WITH "P"!
ARCHIBALD, YOU'RE LASHING OUT
YOU NEED TO APOLOGIZE AND TAKE SOME DEEP, CALMING BREATHS
IF YOU CAN'T DO IT FOR YOURSELF, WILL YOU DO IT FOR THE FATHER OF YOUR COUNTRY?
The Funtime Learning Hour or so is having technical difficulties!
We'll be right back!
ARCHIBALD NO! YOU'RE HURTING PRESIDENT LINCOLN!
TIGER, PLEASE . . . YOU'VE ALREADY BEEN OFF THE AIR FOR FIVE MINUTES, AND THIS IS THE SECOND TIME THE SET'S CAUGHT FIRE
SO JUST PUT THE BASEBALL BAT DOWN . . .
ASSISTANT DIRECTOR
NO! I STILL HAVE FORTY MINUTES LEFT TO FILL WITH P-WORDS!
AND NOBODY GETS TO LEAVE UNTIL WE'VE COVERED ALL OF THEM!
I'VE GOT A P WORD FOR YOU!
K-9
DOES "TACKLE" START WITH P?
YOU'RE THINKING OF "POUNCE"
IF YOU INSIST!
AIR
K-9
WE KNOW YOU'RE IN HERE! EVERY TEN SECONDS YOU DON'T SURRENDER, WE'RE ADDING ANOTHER COUNT OF RESISTING ARREST!
HE'S A DOG, RESISTING ARREST DOESN'T STICK WITH HIM
AWW, BUT THAT'S MY FAVORITE PART
LIGHTS
THIS IS IT . . . THEY'RE TAKING MY SHOW AWAY, MY LAST CHANCE AT RIGHTFUL STARDOM!
BUT HOW CAN YOU ARREST ME WHEN YOU HAVE LIGHTS IN YOUR EYES!
TIGER WAIT! WE HAVEN'T INSTALLED THE VOLTAGE REG--
'PLOSION
HEY HEY HEY! YOU'RE LISTENING TO THE EPILOGUE AFTERNOON ON KPIT WITH SPONGECAKE AND THE CHERRY ON TOP, FILLING IN FOR THE CROM
SOME TRAGIC NEWS, THE MILTON TELEVISION STUDIO HAS EXPLODED!
preeeeeeeeee
THAT'S NOT THE RIGHT-- WHAT'S THE WORD, CHERRY ON TOP?
FORTUNATELY, IT SEEMS EVERYONE WAS INSULATED FROM THE BLAST THANKS TO THE DENSELY-PACKED PLYWOOD SOUND STAGE, AND MANAGED TO ESCAPE WITH ONLY MINOR SCRAPES AND A LOT OF SPLINTERS
THE ONE RESPONSIBLE FOR THE EXPLOSION, TIGER "ARCHIBALD" ARBELT, WAS SENTENCED TO PROBATION AND TOLD HE WAS A "VERY BAD DOG"
SIS, YOU COULD AT LEAST TRY TO USE THE SOUNDBOARD
DUE TO A CONTRACT OVERSIGHT, HOWEVER, HE WAS ONLY FINANCIALLY LIABLE FOR GARNISHED WAGES
ROCK MILTON HAS NO PLANS ON CONTINUING THE SHOW, HOWEVER . . .
THE FUNTIME LEARNING HOUR OR SO HAS BEEN PURCHASED BY A&E FOR 1.4 MILLION DOLLARS
CATCH THE ENTIRE TWELVE-PART MINISERIES ON THIS SUMMER'S REALITY TV LINEUP!
SHAREHOLDERS MEETING
END!

YOU MAKE ME SO HAPPY, KING
AND I KNOW WE'LL BE TOGETHER FOREVER . . .
FOREVER . . .
CLICK
FOREVER . . .
LOW BATT
1:57
O PETE WHO ART IN HEAVEN . . . I HAVE A GREAT BURDEN ON MY MIND, AND I CANNOT BEAR IT ANY LONGER . . .
. . . SO I'M CALLING YOUR BLUFF, MOTHER PHEASANT
Housepets!
Heaven's Not Enough
HERE I AM!
GYAH!
SO WHAT WAS THAT YOU WERE SAYING ABOUT BECOMING MY AVATAR SO YOU CAN REMAIN A DOG FOREVER?
OH NO YOU DON'T! I HAVE YOU FIGURED OUT THIS TIME . . . YOU DON'T NEED ME
. . .
EXCUSE ME?
EVERYTHING I'VE SEEN--THE SHEER SCOPE OF THIS COSMIC GAME--SUGGESTS THAT YOU CAN'T POSSIBLY BE DOWN TO ONE LAST GAMBIT! YOU WON'T SURRENDER, YOU CAN'T SURRENDER! YOUR PRIDE WON'T ALLOW IT!
OH KING, YOU SAD, NAIVE MORTAL . . .
YOU CANNOT FATHOM HOW RIGHT YOU ARE
KING? . . . WHAT'S GOING ON?
CONTRACT
X
AH! BAILEY! I THOUGHT THIS WAS PRIVA-- I MEAN . . . THIS IS ALL A DREAM! BACK TO SLEEP!
QUITE REAL I'M AFRAID
YOU KEEP YOUR BEAK SHUT!
REALLY, IS SILENCE THE ANSWER HERE?
IF YOU KNOW SOMETHING ABOUT THE BIG BLUE GLISTENING HUNK OF A GRYPHON THAT SUDDENLY APPEARED IN YOUR BEDROOM, I BELIEVE YOUR WIFE HAS A RIGHT TO KNOW
KING, PLEASE DO WHAT THE MONSTROUS APPARITION SAYS BEFORE I START SCREAMING UNCONTROLLABLY
I SAID "GLISTENING HUNK"!

THIS IS PETE
HE IS BASICALLY A DEMIGOD, AND HE'S PLAYING A COSMIC GAME THAT USES MORTALS AS THE PLAYING PIECES-- AND I HAPPEN TO BE ONE OF THESE PIECES
SO HE'S BEEN EXTORTING ME FOR THE LAST SEVERAL YEARS TRYING TO FORCE ME TO COOPERATE
NOT PRECISELY EXTORTION SO MUCH AS COLLECTIONS-- HE REALLY DOES OWE ME
YOU LIAR! YOU TORE ME AWAY FROM EVERYTHING AND CAUSED ME NOTHING BUT MISERY!
"QUEENIE" MIGHT NOT SEE IT THAT WAY, STUD
UNLESS SHE'S "THE OL' BATTLE AXE" ALREADY, AND IN ONLY ONE YEAR? MARRIAGE REALLY IS DETERIORATING THESE DAYS
YOU HAD NOTHING TO DO WITH THAT!
THEN ASK HER WHAT SHE'D BE TO YOU WITHOUT ME!
BOTH OF YOU SHUT YOUR BISCUIT HOLES!
AH, NOW I SEE WHAT YOU MEAN
I WILL PLAY BADMINTON WITH YOUR SCISSORED-OFF WINGS, BEAKIE!
I DON'T CARE WHAT PLANET OR OTHERWORLD YOU COME FROM
I DON'T CARE WHAT HE'D BE "WITHOUT YOU"
YOU NEED TO GET OUT
JUST TELL HIM, KING
THERE ISN'T A THING IN THIS WORLD THAT COULD KEEP ME FROM--
I USED TO BE HUMAN, ALRIGHT?!
PETE TURNED ME INTO THIS!
. . . OKAY, WE'VE CLEARLY HIT THE ABSURDITY LIMIT IN THE DREAM, SO I'LL JUST WILL MYSELF AWAKE
BAILEY . . .
IT'S TRUE . . . WHEN I WAS FIRST CHANGED I HATED IT
I WAS CONFUSED AND SCARED--AND BIG BIRD DIDN'T REALLY DO MUCH TO HELP
OH YES I DID
I BELIEVE VERY MUCH THAT CHARACTER IS REFINED THROUGH HARDSHIP
--MORTAL CHARACTER; I DON'T GO FOR THAT STUFF MYSELF
THAT DOESN'T GIVE YOU THE RIGHT TO USE ME!
ARE YOU HAPPY WITH YOUR LIFE, KING?
. . . YES
THEN WHAT'S THE WORRY? ALL YOU NEED TO DO TO KEEP YOUR LIFE AND WIFE IS BECOME MY AVATAR FOR A WHILE, FIGHT FOR ME IN BRUTAL COMBAT, FOLLOW MY EVERY BIDDING--
YOU KNOW, SOMETIMES I WONDER IF YOU'RE BEING REASONABLE, BUT THEN--
MAYBE I JUST BELIEVE IN FULL DISCLOSURE
BUT YOU'D BE LYING
AND THAT WOULD BE UNBECOMING OF ME!
SO . . . IF YOU DON'T GET AN AVATAR TO FIGHT FOR YOU . . . YOU TURN KING BACK INTO A HUMAN, AND THIS ALL GOES AWAY?
CORRECTION, THE SPELL EXPIRES ON ITS OWN
WHATEVER!
KING . . . UNDERSTAND WHEN I SAY "I LOVE YOU" I DO NOT SAY IT LIGHTLY
I KNOW, BUT I CAN'T JUST--
TAKE ME INSTEAD!
BAILEY NO!
I HAVE TO HAND IT TO YOU KING . . .
YOU REALLY KNOW HOW TO TRANSFORM PITY INTO DEVOTION . . .
CONTRACT

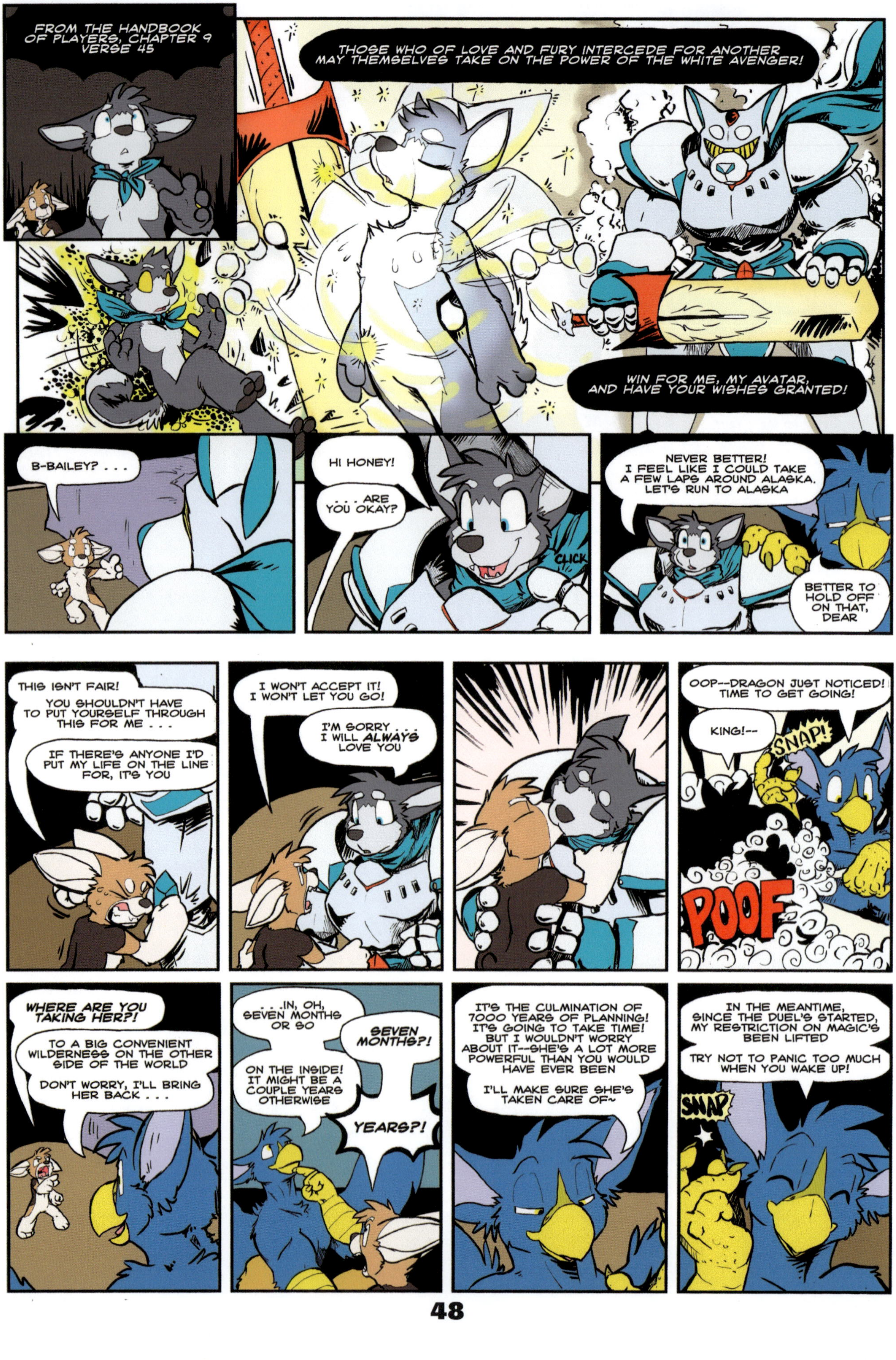
FROM THE HANDBOOK OF PLAYERS, CHAPTER 9 VERSE 45
THOSE WHO OF LOVE AND FURY INTERCEDE FOR ANOTHER MAY THEMSELVES TAKE ON THE POWER OF THE WHITE AVENGER!
WIN FOR ME, MY AVATAR, AND HAVE YOUR WISHES GRANTED!
B-BAILEY? . . .
HI HONEY!
. . . ARE YOU OKAY?
CLICK
NEVER BETTER! I FEEL LIKE I COULD TAKE A FEW LAPS AROUND ALASKA. LET'S RUN TO ALASKA
BETTER TO HOLD OFF ON THAT, DEAR
THIS ISN'T FAIR!
YOU SHOULDN'T HAVE TO PUT YOURSELF THROUGH THIS FOR ME . . .
IF THERE'S ANYONE I'D PUT MY LIFE ON THE LINE FOR, IT'S YOU
I WON'T ACCEPT IT! I WON'T LET YOU GO!
I'M SORRY . . . I WILL ALWAYS LOVE YOU
OOP--DRAGON JUST NOTICED! TIME TO GET GOING!
KING!--
SNAP!
POOF
WHERE ARE YOU TAKING HER?!
TO A BIG CONVENIENT WILDERNESS ON THE OTHER SIDE OF THE WORLD
DON'T WORRY, I'LL BRING HER BACK . . .
. . .IN, OH, SEVEN MONTHS OR SO
SEVEN MONTHS?!
ON THE INSIDE! IT MIGHT BE A COUPLE YEARS OTHERWISE
YEARS?!
IT'S THE CULMINATION OF 7000 YEARS OF PLANNING! IT'S GOING TO TAKE TIME! BUT I WOULDN'T WORRY ABOUT IT--SHE'S A LOT MORE POWERFUL THAN YOU WOULD HAVE EVER BEEN
I'LL MAKE SURE SHE'S TAKEN CARE OF~
IN THE MEANTIME, SINCE THE DUEL'S STARTED, MY RESTRICTION ON MAGIC'S BEEN LIFTED
TRY NOT TO PANIC TOO MUCH WHEN YOU WAKE UP!
SNAP

Panel 1
Fox: I'M HERE... WHAT'S THE EMERGENCY?
Bailey: KING DIDN'T SAY-- HE'S IN HIS ROOM AND SAID NOBODY SHOULD COME IN BUT YOU
HUFF

Panel 2
Fox: KING? WHERE'S BAILEY?
King: =SIGH= YEAH, ABOUT THAT...

Panel 3
Fox: KING, YOU LOOK LIKE A FAT CARTOON ESKIMO
King: FUNNY YOU SHOULD MENTION MY *APPEARANCE*...

Panel 4
Fox: I DON'T KNOW HOW MUCH YOU NEED ME TO REASSURE YOU-- *WHATEVER* YOU HAPPEN TO LOOK LIKE, I AM PREPARED FOR IT
I DON'T BELIEVE YOU, BUT I DON'T THINK THERE'S MUCH ELSE I CAN DO TO PREPARE YOU, SO...

Panel 5
Fox: ...KING?

Panel 7
King: TOLD YOU SO
Fox: OH, SHUT UP...

Panel 8
Fox: FIDO, WE NEED TO SPEAK WITH SABRINA. IT'S *URGENT*
Fido: WHO'S THE--
Fox: THAT'S NOT IMPORTANT RIGHT NOW!

Panel 9
Fido: WELL I'M SORRY, YOU JUST MISSED HER; SHE LEFT EARLY THIS MORNING WITH SOMETHING IMPORTANT TO DO
...BUT SHE *DID* LEAVE THIS NOTE AND SAID ONLY YOU SHOULD READ IT, IF YOU'RE WITH A HUMAN
WAS KINDA STRANGE, BUT THAT'S SABRINA
Fox: FIGURES

Panel 10
Note: "FIDO, SWEETIE, YOU BETTER NOT BE READING THIS OR I'M SICING THE JAGUAR GHOST ON YOU. HUGS N KISSES. FOX, KING, GO TO THE SANDWICH HOUSE."
King: SANDWICH HOUSE? TAROT WAS PEANUT'S GIRLFRIEND--IF SHE'S LEFT, I REALLY DON'T WANT TO KNOW WHAT CONDITION HE'S IN...

Panel 11
Peanut: HEY GUYS! COME IN AND HAVE SOME SNACKS! ALSO, TAROT TOLD ME TO GIVE YOU A THING THAT I DON'T KNOW WHAT IT IS
Fox: IT'S WORSE THAN I FEARED

TAROT TOLD ME I WASN'T TO GIVE THIS THING TO YOU UNTIL THE THING SHE WAS GOING TO DO WITH DRAGON AND SABRINA HAPPENED, BECAUSE UNLESS THAT HAPPENED THEN THIS THING WAS GOING TO HAPPEN WOULD HAPPEN DIFFERENTLY THAN IT HAS HAPPENED, IN WHICH CASE THIS THING WOULD HAPPEN DIFFERENTLY
I DON'T FOLLOW
HERE, I GIVE YOU THING
WHAT IS IT?
I DUNNO. SOME MAGIC THING. TAROT HAS TONS OF THEM, BUT THIS ONE IS YOURS AND MR. DOGSMELL'S
WELL THAT'S NOT VERY HELPFUL IF WE DON'T--
JOEL ROBINSON, I AM HERE FOR YOUR SOUL!
AAAAAH!
OR MORE SPECIFICALLY, FOR THE PART OF YOUR SOUL THAT IS YOUR FATE. DO YOU HAVE IT ON YOU?
YOU DID THAT ON PURPOSE!
BUT OF COURSE!
WHAT ARE YOU DOING?
JUST SNIFFING
WHY HERE, WHY NOW?!
WHY DIDN'T YOU WARN ME?!
IT WAS A PERSONAL FAVOR THAT WE DELAYED UNTIL YOU HAD THAT TOTEM
TELLING YOU WOULD HAVE CHANGED YOUR ACTIONS AND THEIR OUTCOME
YOU MEAN YOU DELAYED PICKING UP MY FATE JUST SO YOU COULD DOVETAIL IT WITH ANOTHER CELESTIAL PLAN!?
CERTAINLY; WE MINIMIZED THE WAIT SO THIS WOULD BE AS PAINLESS AS POSSIBLE FOR YOU
I'VE BEEN AT MY WIT'S END ABOUT THAT ACCURSED THING FOR YEARS!!
. . . RIGHT, THAT'S WHY WE ONLY WAITED A LITTLE WHILE
SEE, THIS CONVERSATION RIGHT HERE IS WHY I HATE TALKING WITH DEMIGODS
HERE, TAKE IT--AND TELL WHOEVER YOU'RE WORKING FOR THAT THEY CAN GO TO--WELL, I'M PRETTY SURE YOU'RE MORE FAMILIAR WITH THE PLACE THAN I
TELL THEM YOURSELF. YOU HAVE ADDITIONALLY BEEN GRANTED AN AUDIENCE IN HEAVEN
THE VIP TREATMENT, NO LESS! FULL PACKAGE--NOT BOUND BY TIME NOR SPACE NOR PHYSICAL NEED! BRING ALONG A FRIEND!
OH REALLY . . . AND THEY'LL ANSWER TO MY DEMANDS?
VISIT BEAUTIFUL HEAVEN
DO NOT FORGET YOUR PLACE, HUMAN. WE WILL DO WHAT WE CAN--BUT YOU MUST DO YOUR PART FIRST
FOX? . . .
I COULD USE A VACATION
THEN COME
HEAVEN AWAITS
PLEASE KEEP YOUR HANDS, ARMS AND IMMORTAL SOULS INSIDE THE STAIRWAY AT ALL TIMES!
TO BE CONTINUED . . .

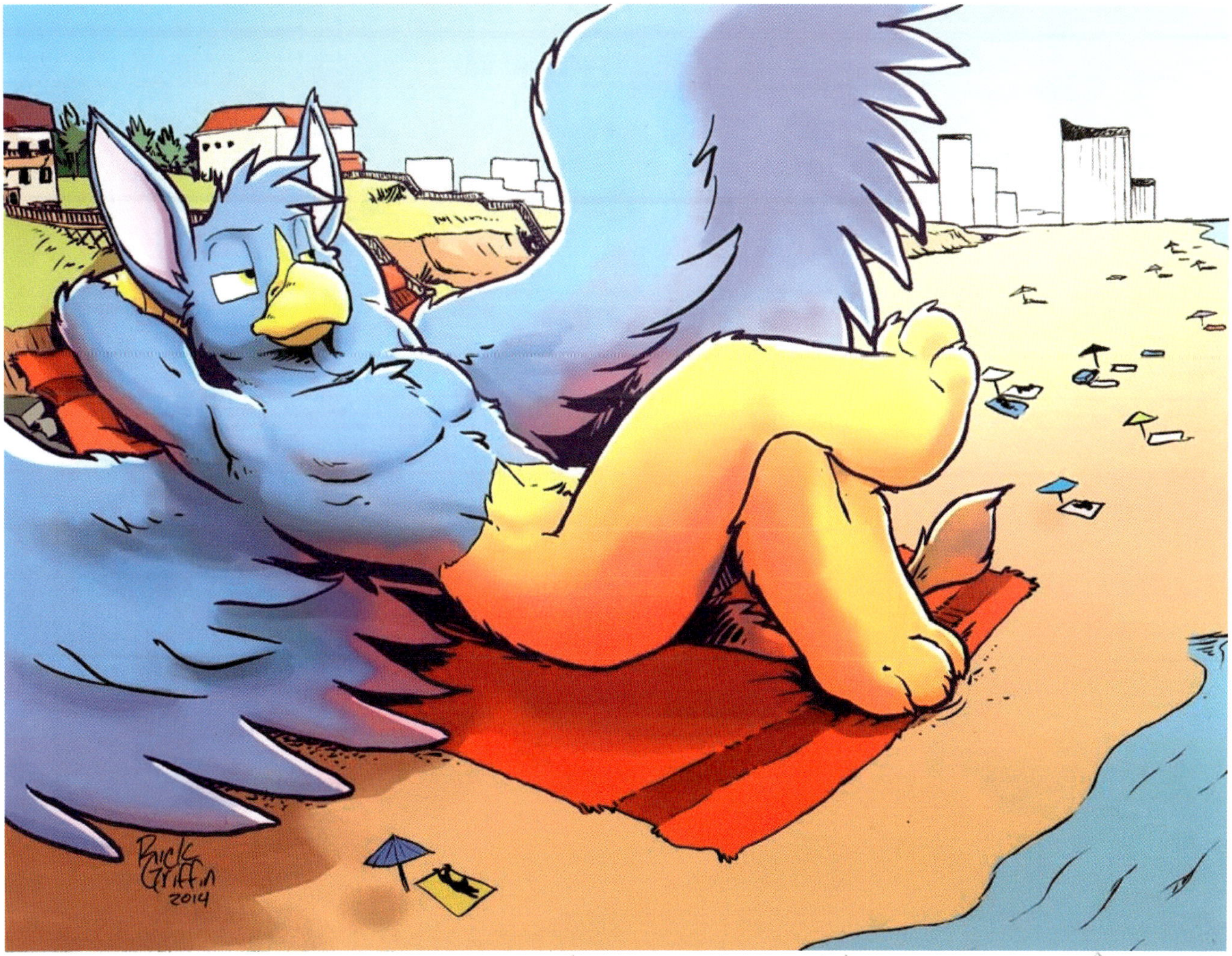
Rick Griffin 2014

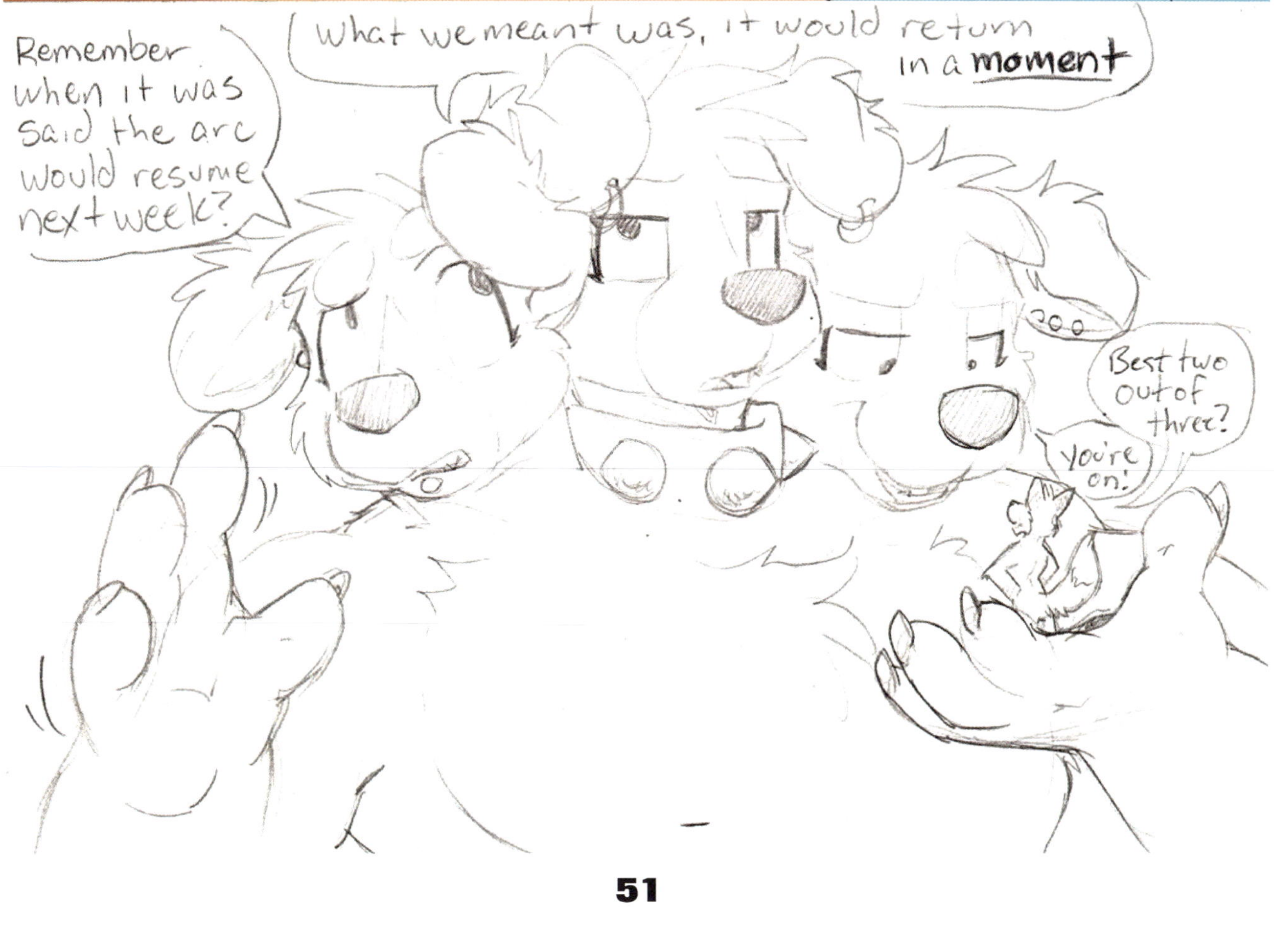
Remember when it was said the arc would resume next week?
What we meant was, it would return in a **moment**
zoo
Best two out of three?
You're on!

Next time, on
Housepets!

--ECT

MOTHER OF DOG

MEANWHILE

ALL HAIL GEORGE BAILEY, WHO SITS ON THE THRONE OF SANTA!

YEAH, WOO-HOO